HOLLANDIA NOVA, 1712
Song of the Coast

N.B.J.Clayton

Warning!

Kulinma! Ngulakujaku-kula!
This book might contain names of people who have since
departed this world.

Publication data:

HOLLANDIA NOVA, 1712 - Song of the Coast, 1ˢᵗ ed.
ISBN: 978-0-6487672-7-5

DRA012000   Drama/Australian & Oceanian
FIC014000   Fiction/Historical/General
POE010000   Poetry/Australian & Oceanian

A BRIEF NOTE ON HISTORY

The Dutch United East India Company (Vereenigde Oost-Indische Compagnie – VOC) was the most powerful company at the time of the Zuytdorp, and the Zuytdorp was one of their largest ships. A great monopoly stretched from Holland to Asia (namely Batavia [Jakarta] where the VOC headquarters was established) and other countries which were a source of great wealth and commodity. Within time the VOC boasted settlements in Java, Sumatra, Borneo, India, Ceylon, Arabia, Persia, Bengal, Malacca, Celebs, Timor, China and Japan. Trade between these centres was also of strategic importance: where trade and wealth was concerned. Copper, tin, spices, opium and dyes were the basic requisites of commerce.

Spices were something new to Europe, tantalizing fragments of a whole that inspired great satisfaction within all across the country, each and every one tired of the tasteless morsels dished out at dinner time, turning to spices like a tidal wave upon a beach.

It was usual for more than one ship to be in the company on another and eight months forecast for the voyage ahead, being provided the mandatory and rather necessary rest stop at the Cape of Good Hope, Table Bay, for a period of ten days, a period of time which had been cut drastically from an extravagant three to four weeks. There was a fort here, established in 1652 for the sole purpose of providing medical aid and stores. A hospital of 200 beds saw many stationed upon the seafaring ships take harbour within the facility to fight that dreaded scourge of the seas, scurvy, so it was common knowledge that many hands would exchange places, those that had commenced a journey from Holland not necessarily completing the trip with that posting; it was another sad fact that all had to face and that was the death rate for those on such a long voyage, for quite a large portion of the ship's company would come to grief and be launched into the sea covered in sacking; pickings for oceanic life.

To avoid the dangers of the coast, from Table Bay to Batavia, at a time when the Portuguese were an enemy to be avoided, an alternate route was discovered: which also alleviated the problems in regards to wind direction. The ships would travel due west for approximately 1,000 Dutch miles before turning north. It was unfortunate for the time, however, that there was no means by which to accurately determine longitude at sea, latitude on the other hand was quite reliable. Eventually land was encountered and this then became the accepted method of voyage: to seek the sight of land and then head north towards the coast of Sumatra. For almost a hundred years sailors were fortunate enough to cast their eyes upon the west coast of a great mass of land, thought to have been part of New Guinea. Many names were cast upon the landmass, eventually Hollandia Nova taking hold. Only one real warning of impending danger was forecast to the captains of these ships and that was to avoid the Triall Rocks [Tryal Rocks - off the north-west coast of Australia] as the submerged capacity of the hidden encumbrance was enough to see a ship easily bashed, sliced, and quartered.

The Zuytdorp was the largest ship within the VOC and only two others were of equal size. It was built between 23 Dec 1700 and 22 June 1701, being 160 feet long, 40 feet wide, and the depth of the hold was 17 feet (283 millimetres to the Amsterdam foot). She was capable of carrying 250 lasts (500 tons) which towards the latter portion of her life was increased on paper and task: the Zuytdorp in 1712 carried in the vicinity of 576 lasts.

The Zuytdorp, due to the situation with war and pirates, carried ten 12-pound guns, twenty-two 8-pound guns and eight 4-pound guns (swivel cannons). The swivel and two 8-pounders were made of bronze; all others were iron muzzle loaders.

The Zuytdorp and Belvliet had set sail for the Cape of Good Hope, to journey for most of the voyage within sight of one another, but there were instances where they were to become separated, for one reason or another. The voyage was treacherous to say the least; a longer than expected journey being suffered as the ships had to sail up and around Scotland in order to avoid English ships of the sea patrolling the Channel.

The Zuytdorp arrived at the Cape of Good Hope on 23rd March 1712, and of the original 286 crew had lost 112 men and had 22 sick on board; eight having deserted at São Tomé; most deaths were attributed to scurvy but others of tropical malaria from São Tomé itself. The Belvliet fared little better, percentage wise, and arrived on 27th March, and from a crew of 164 had lost 60 dead and 18 sick, with two desertions at São Tomé.

Much time was then spent at the Cape to replenish men and stores when finally, on 22 April 1712, the Zuytdorp departed the Cape with the ship Kockenge; the Belvliet departing several weeks later on the 9th May.

The Zuytdorp pulled ahead of the Kockenge due to her being a much larger and faster vessel, a vessel of the first class, 200 'eaters' (people) on board, 80-90 of them being new to the ship. And as many do, the skipper decided to sail until sighting land before turning north for Sunda Strait, to take good advantage of the winds which presented themselves.

GENERAL NOTE

There was no single, homogeneous Aboriginal society, but around 250 different tribes and well in excess of 100 different dialects spoken, the difference between the languages [in some cases] being as different as English compared to Portuguese. With such a vast network of tribal backgrounds and varying ceremonial beliefs, where interaction between groups was a common occurrence, it is not surprising to see that members of a tribe were multilingual and able to quite effectively speak 10 different dialects or more.

The differences between tribes were as different as chalk and cheese: their language was different; their customs, kinship systems, ceremonial music and dance... all had its place.

Where subtle interaction was sought between the different clans in order to pursue marriage, partners for boys coming of adulthood and of girls ready to enter into sacred ceremony, groups were bonded by belief and enactment. New myths could hence be strung, beliefs exchanged, strategies of the hunt and food gathering techniques discussed. A cycle of life and survival was maintained and the gene pool stirred well to prevent the curse-of-ancestors from rising from the dead.

There is also one other aspect of aboriginal life which must be made quite clear, and it certainly isn't considered normal, and that is in respect to the genes. There is evidence [in the 20th Century] to show that Aboriginals of the Shark Bay area suffer from Porphyria Variegate, a gene mutation that is traceable to the Dutch, as is the disease in South Africa where 1 in 300 persons suffer from it. It is uncommon and rare, and there is no reason, other than the coupling of an Aboriginal with a survivor of the Zuytdorp, that currently explains the disease being discovered in Australia.

But for the most part there was peace amongst the Aboriginals, right across the land.

In 1623, Jan Carstenz placed colourful descriptions to several armed encounters with the Aboriginals. He spoke of how arid the land was, of how inhospitable and barren the entire place was, where no such horrid place existed anywhere else on earth. He spoke of the inhabitants as the most wretched and poorest that he had ever seen. These comments were carried quite literally back to the Netherlands, and the Dutch government decided that the land was not suitable for colonisation and no benefit could be won from seeking such an endeavour.

It is not surprising therefore that all the men and women that saw the land from far out upon the ocean felt the fear build up within them, a fear suddenly drowned by the so deeply satisfying and secure feeling within, in both knowledge and thought, that they would never have to set foot upon such a miserable place.

And then one day a ship approached this horrid place, its crew unaware of what was about to become of them, for the Zuytdorp had ventured too close to land....

AUTHOR'S NOTE:

Off the coast of Western Australia lies the Indian Ocean. To aid in the writing of this poem I shall often refer to these waters as 'sea'.

PROLOGUE

In 1829 the Swan River Colony was founded, hundreds strong,
A community as many other, settlers endeavouring no wrong,
Founded within short years upon the east Australian coast,
A land so bountiful, gifts for the plucking, much to boast.

The name Swan River, derived from that which it was christened,
By the Dutch, many decades before, as it so happened,
When black swans upon the river evoked a stirring of affection,
A beauty which men saw, feeling that natural connection.

So beautiful these swans were, much beauty well stack,
That they were drawn from the river and taken back,
A visual feast to be well endowed, a gift, a pleasure,
Shown well to the government and the people in good measure.

Just five years later and two aboriginals could be seen,
Within this district, walking leisurely but seeming keen,
Steady walking pace to see them delivered with spear in hand,
No hateful thought within them, of great tolerance, of good brand.

They were Tonquin and Weenat, lean, tall and dark,
Their darkened flesh unmistakable, eyes alight with spark,
Rather beautiful when it comes to the point of features,
Worthy and of great characteristics, with the desert no fractures.

HOLLANDIA NOVA, 1712

Their faces were alive, a calmness and spring to walk,
Walking silently, looking about them, no need to talk,
A living script to the aboriginals, whom with the land did live,
A semblance to nature itself, and their people that did give.

The very structure of the skin and bone, their faces so undulating,
Skin and large noses that appeared to sit flat, to face much doting,
A reasonable testimony to a life well lived, one so gifted,
Life shared with nature and the land itself, seemingly related.

They had come to terms with white man, having settled from afar,
The way in which they hence founded, whites, a roaming star,
This wonderment of difference permeating this land so free,
They seemed peaceful, but the aborigines would not give a knee.

And so Tonquin and Weenat had something to offer,
Some information that may be of interest to these men, not master,
To provide information on a shipwreck that had come their way,
To offer courtesy for wad of tobacco, a comfort to have this day.

Such information must be worth a little to these people so new,
Considering it was a white man's ship, sunk amidst ocean mew,
One smashed badly upon rocks some forty miles north of Kalbarri,
But their information was stark, misconstrued, hazy and glary.

Passed down from tribe to tribe, from elder to young,
Carried to sacred meeting, their corroboree well sung,
From other meetings to meeting where wives are won,
From hunting ground to hunting ground where speers stung.

The police officer sat rigid behind his desk before relaxing a little,
The story quite tense, but he listened, before him set his vittle,
The sentences delivered his ears missing words here and there,
The jest of the story is noted for what it was before confused stare.

There is a shipwreck to the north, a thirty day walk,
In the land of the Malgana, and they continue to talk,
Where the tribe Wayle lives off the land in pleasant solitude,
Visiting this place of wreck amidst curious attitude.

There is much money, that has been washed upon hard rock,
The officer imitates them a little, to understand, not to mock,
Silver coins that are so thick in the water, sand so hard to see,
So thick that it is ankle deep in places, a place so wild but free.

The ship has broken up into three main parts, this its grave,
A three-mast ship that will never again roll upon the wave,
But it also resembles much more than a pile of rubble,
A story hard to fathom, hard to piece together, hard to cobble.

Tonquin and Weenat look the officer up and down,
He takes his notes, writing amidst occasional frown,
Storing notes on the main points of the story,
Points of greater interest, awaiting him much glory.

They continue with their story of how the tall white men fell,
From the wreck and then upon the land, a little more to tell,
They are taken by the aboriginals where courtesy is exchanged,
A lasting relationship scored, relationships hence arranged.

HOLLANDIA NOVA, 1712

The officer displays another frown, missing interpretation,
Thinking the wreck is most recent, ready for his administration,
Not considering for a moment that this is old information,
No clear understanding that he is scribing 122 year old dictation.

And further still, both Tonquin and Weenat provide advice,
That the white men lived in little houses, strangely nice,
Lived around three fires, dwellings made of canvas and wood,
And not so very far from the face of the cliff, here they stood.

The police officer must act quickly, provide aid to those in need,
A rescue prepared, to save these people, despite his inner greed,
Not knowing that nought will be found of any survivor,
Unless remains are so dug from the site, a site of ill-favour.

THE BREAKING

The 5th of June, 1712, on board the Zuytdorp are 286 souls,
174 seamen including those of higher rank, of many roles,
100 soldiers, 4 tradesmen and 8 passengers and stores,
Almost all will perish, washed upon unsavoury shores.

It came upon the men, women and children without warning,
A voice upon the wind coming closer, an incessant whining,
A great calamity that fell upon them in the dead of night,
The sky above was as dark as one had ever known, of no delight.

Intermittent sparks of light throwing themselves upon the world,
The decking and masts of ship lighting up, strength so hurled,
The savage wind and rain catching them unaware,
Thunder and lightning, together, striking out, so unfair.

The sheer force of nature stole people's voices away,
No verbal sound herald to ear amidst the heinous fray,
Shouts and screams on deck broken up by the wind,
Gone even garbled sound from bodies of terrified mind.

Crew members on deck continued throwing themselves to duty,
The last thing most would do in this storm of ill-fate, no beauty,
And upon their minds was the pressure to be successful,
To gift upon their endeavours a victory, to be eternally grateful.

HOLLANDIA NOVA, 1712

The eight passengers below deck huddled together,
Bound by the horror of this most beastly weather,
The culminating of fear, the worst ever experienced before,
This journey to Batavia now sour, what more was in store.

And several oil lamps, secured upon hooks, alight and frail,
Swung back and forth, as the ship rocked, swinging upon nail,
Frightful looks all around them without doubt,
As shadows moved here and there, all about.

Three were wives heading to Batavia, to meet with husband,
A child in each of their arms, upon voyage to place so grand,
Fathers to see their child for the first time ever,
Men of high station, most important, earning much stiver.

There was another here, a man of which a lot was known,
But nothing of his younger life or from beginnings what town,
Heading to Batavia to work, a decision made of mind so strong,
To another country so far away, a decision made, now wrong.

Yes indeed, such a grand position advertised at home,
Of bookkeeper profession, of intelligence, not a [archaic] mome,
One to tax his mind to the limits of his skill and knowledge,
For him to work hard and establish good rapport, his pledge.

There was one other, a child of fourteen, in hammock he rests,
Older than the others cradled safely close to mothers' breasts,
He was alone, but did have a minder, that was the bookkeeper,
Who maintained vigil upon this boy who looked like a pauper.

The boy's name was Willem Steyns and of poor situation,
Cast upon an ill wind to carry him amidst his frustration,
To take him far and wide, until the limits of the earth,
To this new country unheard of, different than place of birth.

He was set forth by a poorly mother, a drunken, wretched curse,
She worthy of nought but the little money carried within purse,
He being cast aside by her, for him to be attended to by his father,
Who was a merchant in Batavia, of spices he did gather.

He was a lean man and worked hard to make a wage,
Ensuring much was dispatched to his wife from his cage,
Hands tied in this, a forced vocation, his only learned ability,
Unaware of wife's true state, so few letters received of surety.

He wasn't aware that Willem was on his way to seek him,
For the letter dispatched by wife was carried by the boy so slim,
Months and months on end spent in dreary isolation,
This on top of the dreary company he kept at his station.

The man, as tall as he was fair, tried to give comfort,
A little solace, some spirit, and that was no easy effort,
For the noise and raucous above their heads, on deck,
Continued unabated, furious activity they could not check.

And as the poor boy thought on matters he knew little about,
Fifty per cent of the crew raced upon deck, under threat and shout,
All trying their hardest to put to right the wrong,
Amidst a growing storm of great ferocity, so strong.

HOLLANDIA NOVA, 1712

But let's jump back a little, to the man here within belly,
Within the hold of the ship Zuytdorp, so rotten and smelly,
His name was Pieter Pelsaert, 34 years of age,
Soon to be looked upon, to be the centre of stage.

The passengers were the luckiest of all those on board,
Within the best part of the ship, despite lack of luxury and accord,
Each scared to the core and not fully understanding the truth,
Sailors praying for the light of day, no need to be a sleuth.

Pieter had come to know the three women and Willem rather well,
Had spent the voyage strapped to their every yarn, under a spell,
Every piece of gossip silently taken in and savoured,
An assortment of characters, strongly flavoured.

He was a listener,
Not a talker,
A mover,
Not a loiterer.

As though herald to hear what each had to say,
Sometimes from within the shadows he would stay,
As they talked on their lives and the captain of the ship,
Of the crew and their misdemeanours, and sailors' lip.

They were thrown together in an area away from the main body,
A body of sole function, to work the ship well, not be shoddy,
The seamen whose job it was to see ship's cargo endowed,
To have it ported to dock in Batavia, no lenience allowed.

Pieter saw one of the women fall aside,
Atop her baby of just 14 months, as though to hide,
The babies face blue and crimson, the ocean a menace,
Resembling a mix of darkened sky and heated furnace.

He reached out to give aid,
To help up this stricken maid,
To offer solace for just a moment,
Pieter quick to action but not stringent.

"My God," Pieter bellowed into the woman's ear,
As he pulled her up from floor, into eyes did peer,
"What manner of transgression forced you to attend this voyage,
With one so young, to force your life to ocean and its rage?"

As Pieter picked them up upon rocking wave, he realised his tact,
For the woman felt as though she had be scolded, despite the fact,
And then the woman sobbed, looking at the man so kind,
Then down into the dead eyes of the one she held, no life to find.

Pieter's mouth dropped, life was truly riding upon a fine thread,
Said Willemtgen, most heartbroken, "My boy; he's dead."
She peered down again upon the form of flesh,
Pulled into her, a tightened grip, that their bodies would mesh.

So tight the hold, the child would never be pried loose,
Amidst raging storm, tossing of ship, no choice to choose,
The tears streamed from her face and Pieter tried to comfort,
Put an arm around her, with true conviction and little effort.

HOLLANDIA NOVA, 1712

The other ladies looked upon the scene,
And then to their own young, love so keen,
Ariaantje with her 18 month old girl, used to laughter,
And Willemyntje with her 4 year old daughter.

Suddenly the door burst open and a seaman appeared,
Ariaen Leyden by name, it never, ever to be smeared,
Out of the darkness and into the light,
Fluctuating oil lamps illuminating his fright.

Shadows moved round,
Eerie shadows to be found,
The Zuytdorp creaked and groaned,
It bellowed, it cried and moaned.

"Pieter, Pieter, quickly man, we need you! All hands to deck,
NOW PIETER! All hands needed or we are a wreck."
And with more suddenness than the man, never to surrender,
The entire ship shuddered that unthinkable, evil shudder.

A noise from beneath her hull did grind and tear,
The most heinous ever heard, to heart a spear,
The entire vessel shifted upon axis, the stern drifting,
As though trying to overtake the bow, sinking and lifting.

Swinging around to port,
Vessel unable to abort,
Rocky seabed to report,
Work to be made short.

Of the damage being caused there was no remorse,
A rocky shoreline platform, of man, soon a [archaic] corse,
And the platform did crunch and grind,
The most heinous place to wreck, to find.

It was a platform to sit between rock and hard place,
Dwarfing the cliff either side with much ill-grace,
Much distemper displayed upon its sullen face,
Almost gone, all traces of survival in this race.

A race for survival, one to hold dear,
Far north and south the cliff does steer,
As far as the eye can see by day,
Rock, upon rock, upon rock, to flay.

The fear within the eyes of the women is one of sheer grief,
Their distorted faces of horror painting a picture of no relief,
Each clutched ever more the little ones so close to them now,
Willemtgen too, embraced hers with great vigour, never to bow.

Death was a strange thing,
Bad gift, Death to bring,
Some accepted it most freely,
Others refuting, seemingly [archaic] seely.

"We're going!" yelled Ariaen as he fell heavily from the doorway,
Knocking his head heavily upon the mast of the ship as he sway,
A mast penetrating all decks of the Zuytdorp, firm and secure,
Most rigid, unflexing, unlike fishing rod bending with lure.

HOLLANDIA NOVA, 1712

And with great ease and horrible wrenching the mast did snap,
Enough to wake even the devil, deep down, asleep or in nap,
From just above the deck it fell away with the rigging,
Unfurled sail falling with it, rope cores ripping.

The Zuytdorp' short sail amidst of an early winter storm,
Lost all integrity, lost all semblance, all form,
This big, square-rigged ship, men forgetting its nativity,
The pending disaster unavoidable, a situation of great gravity.

Soon to be junk,
A mass, a chunk,
Gone the days of varnish,
The ocean now to tarnish.

Men upon the deck were thrown overboard, starboard and lee,
Gifted slow and fast deaths, each to the mercy of the sea,
But little mercy was received this night,
For the vast, vast majority, no more first light.

Barrels and crates, once secured, now rolled around the decking,
Cargo in the hold shifted suddenly, from slumber, now waking,
All aiding the abrupt shifting of the Zuytdorp towards disaster,
Gone all taming, hello calamitous, abrupt end, now the master.

The rats below deck rushed to find safe quarter,
Looking to save themselves from slaughter,
For even the most vile of life did thirst for life,
Did all they could to avoid much strife.

The Zuytdorp carried within her a great quantity of merchandise,
Precious metals, great wealth in the form of silver: most wise,
Coins being its largest hoard,
But much else here on board.

Coins in their thousands; Dutch ducatons, guilders,
Schillings, rix dollars, double stuivers and stuivers,
Spanish pieces of eight, pieces of four and pieces of two,
Spanish-Netherlands ducatons and patagons, thrown from view.

There was also gold which came in the form of Dutch ducats,
And many, many ingots of silver, amidst rat-chasing cats,
Such great quantities of wealth and riches carried in chests,
Packed and secured, hiding from view the rodent nests.

Two locks saw to it that each chest was bolted secure,
Each nailed down with sail cloth, to escape desire and lure,
Stored within the captain's cabin, below the poop,
Much more room and comfort than forborne sloop.

More luxury here for the captain,
But now gone the luxury and fashion,
Soon to go the silver coins valued at 248,886 guilders,
Gone 100,000 of newly-minted schillings and double stuivers.

But she also carried other commodities,
Needles, muskets and blunderbusses,
Lead, linseed, bacon, nothing on which to sneer,
She was filled to the brim with barrels of wine and beer.

HOLLANDIA NOVA, 1712

1,813 pounds of fresh meat, ten live sheep, salt, pitch, paper,
Vegetables, potherbs, 2 hundredweight of beans, rope, copper,
2 hundredweight of peas, 300 pounds of rice, plates, sulphur,
Oils, cloth, canvas, sail yarn, medical stores, butter and leather.

And what good was all of this? It was ambition,
It was enterprise, for wealth, its ammunition,
Sanctioned from the hull of this grand ship, beneath every hatch,
And then Zuytdorp's return to Europe with an even bigger catch.

To return with spices, salt, pepper, textiles, china, silks and cotton,
Tea, coffee, nutmeg, cloves, cinnamon, mace: nothing forgotten,
All from Batavia and around, from this town,
And with anything else that could be tied down.

Damn it; damn it all, all to be wasted; on a ship no one can steer,
It was all loose, being thrown helplessly around, there and here,
Impossible to avoid the doom, whether below deck or upon it,
Men broken, being killed, made of flesh and bone, not granite.

Broken arms, broken noses, broken souls and mind,
Then heard the sudden call, snatched by the wind,
"Every man for himself", a call most dire,
Save yourself if you can, before life does retire.

And no sooner than being called by the man aloft,
He was speared by flying debris in gut of flesh, so soft,
As another of the ship's masts snapped and fell upon the decking,
The ship pitched further off its axis, far from soul-saving bearing.

Forced further upon unforgiving rock,
Into mind you cannot take stock,
It is surreal, nothing you can imagine,
A reality of horror, many shivers up a spine.

The Zuytdorp gives way to further, sudden bouts of lurching,
Upon the starboard side of ship, huge waves of terror thrashing,
Water now flowing freely within the hull,
No hope in altering the course, from it to pull.

Everyone trying to save themselves from the torments of the sea,
A time of few minutes for one thought only: to be free, to be free,
No time now to reflect upon anything except all manner of escape,
Each endeavour to disallow the heinous rock its merciless rape.

Pieter makes answer to the call, takes it as a command to act,
A call to duty, one not wished but he needed to react,
A hidden desire not to leave anyone behind,
Not to leave anyone here, upon the rocks to grind.

He could not leave an helpless woman with child,
Be the child dead or alive, the woman was mild,
Or the child known as Willem, he could not spurn,
For him there was life, much of it to learn.

"Quickly, Willem; you have to help me," and Pieter stumbled,
The shifting of the ship, grinding on its bottom, it rumbled,
And then further groans, mayhem being voiced from every fibre,
Further groans of mayhem being voiced in resonance and timbre.

HOLLANDIA NOVA, 1712

The ship's core commenced to bend, to split,
The sound of cracking wood, integrity to quit,
The penetration of sound deep into their ears,
So loud, hardly believed, as the devil jeers.

"What do I do!" said Willem, the fright upon his face does grate,
Written in bold, the bulging eyes giving rise to the frantic state,
His near shattered mind and nerve. "Tell me, Pieter; please."
All this whilst the breaking of ship does continue to tease,

Pieter could not deny that the boy's frame of mind scared him,
To his wits end his feelings endeavoured to betray and to trim,
As though whittling his very fabric, a threat to characteristic,
But Pieter did react as a true man, overcome all to be realistic.

But the boy must be forced to endure and provide assistance,
For only then would he forget the fear within him and commence,
To commence his crawl from the abyss in which they had fallen,
To be brave before all, to grow up, not to be overly sullen.

"Give aid to Willemtgen and her son, do it now, no time to waste,
I'll attend Ariaantje and Willemyntje," said Pieter in haste,
And as Willem's mouth began to open, a movement at his brow,
Pieter added further, quite abruptly, so urgent: "Quickly, now!"

"Please, Willemtgen," said Willem, attaching his tether,
"Take hold of my arm and we'll scale the steps together."
Willemtgen's face showed a glare of hope then and there,
Even with her dead son still in her arms, so much to bear.

Willemtgen then reached out to grab hold of the boy,
A man to grow from one so young, strength to deploy,
At the same instant the worst thing to happen did transpire,
A monstrously huge wave struck the ship, all of it, the entire.

It broke into three pieces, hit hard by tremendous force,
Hitting the starboard side of the Zuytdorp without remorse,
But a wave has no feelings, no action to check or feel,
But Poseidon and the devil would provide a different spiel.

The bow broke away, 22 feet of her, and shifted 60 feet,
Towards the shoreline platform, many boulders there to meet,
With their bone-breaking knobs and points awaiting its delivery,
To gnaw upon it as man gnaws upon steak, gifting great quivery.

The stern headed in a most forward motion,
Towards a part of the shoreline, the nearest portion,
Delivered just 28 feet away from the main bulk of the ship,
To the base of this cliff, upon its very lower lip.

It broke up a little, steadying herself upon the rocks, it slowed,
Some 53 feet of her in which all the treasure on board was stowed,
The centre most portion, all 85 feet of that which remained,
Rammed home against the platform, no further ground gained.

The fallen mast upon the deck,
Shifted slightly upon the wreck,
Crushing several men looking to survive,
Who applied herculean efforts to stay alive.

HOLLANDIA NOVA, 1712

Those few men that remained upon, or within, drew last breaths,
Within the bow portion of the vessel, died quick and slow deaths,
Broken bones and concussion in situation so serious,
By drowning, flying debris, or simply knocked unconscious.

Trapped within the rigging and unable to move,
Such death traps in the making, the rigging did prove,
And those tumultuous few of the stern fared little better,
But that portion of the ship availed strong character.

Pieter and Willem were both here,
Alongside the females and children so dear,
Companions and other members of the crew,
Some of them, until this day, they never really knew.

The higher the station a sailor of the sea held,
And the more with the upper class he could meld,
Closer to passengers, their sons and daughters,
More closely situated to the door of the captain's quarters.

Other than the skipper himself were the following: master gunner,
Stockmaker, under steersman, bosun; clerk and senior carpenter,
His 2nd and 3rd; upper steersman, master surgeon, bricklayer,
Coppersmith, comforter of the sick, under surgeon, firelock maker.

All were dead, spread throughout the ship, cast out upon the sea,
Dashed upon the rocky coast, pulled beneath the waves so free,
The surmounting weight of wave upon wave crashing about,
Upon their victims amidst callous, noisy and boisterous shout.

Pieter broke free from the ferocity of the ocean as it swelled,
Caving in upon him, encasing him, as though jelled,
Spluttering and gasping for breath in waters and night so swart,
To gain some form of initiative, of his predicament to thwart.

And the shimmering of light cast from lightning,
Gave freely, great clarity, of that which was frightening,
He saw a baby floating close by and then the body of a woman,
And then another body; and fear struck a chord, he not a pagan.

And Willem clawed his way from the bottom of his well,
Breaching the surface of the sea, to be rid of this spell,
With an outstretched arm he reached for the sky,
To seek assurance, to seek aid, to use his eyes to spy.

He was surrounded on three sides by the interior of the ship,
Which he had called home, his abode this long, long trip,
The fourth side was now wide open to the dark night air,
And with cast astonishment he saw a vision, one to declare.

It was as though he could perceive the glory of God,
Caste down upon him as though with a nod,
The opportunity of a lifetime taken into hand,
Before his sight, across the sky arced a band.

With the accompaniment of the lightning strikes he saw more,
Silhouette of the cliffs above, like doom, something in store,
Yes, they looked most evil, there amidst lightning strike,
But a vision of beauty, of promise, something in future to like.

HOLLANDIA NOVA, 1712

"Are you okay, Willem? Are you hurt!" came Pieter from behind,
Shouting at the top of his lungs, Willem not alone, clarity to mind,
The open side of the ship now an open invitation,
For more noise to envelope them both, a great penetration.

"Yes; YES! I'm okay," came the reply and Pieter moved closer,
Towards the boy, the one he had grown a little fond of, no poser,
What you see is what you receive, company so seldom sought,
On a few occasions had lifted his spirits when they were wrought.

Now it was Pieter's job to see to it that the favour was returned,
By saving the child's life [and so, see, he has openly learned],
Remaining by his side in this, their hour of need,
Pieter, bookkeeper, now filled with a duty of care: he agreed.

There was a small gap between the stern and the shoreline,
The platform of rock which was vacant of sand, the coast's spine,
There was no soft landing, no offering of support from nature,
A gap to be breached before thrust against talons of stature.

To speak more than what was required, was wasteful,
At a time when gasps for air were pulled in by the mouthful,
And energy reserves were required to climb to safety,
Here instinct took over sacked bodies of flesh in their entirety.

Pieter closed the small gap towards the boy and grabbed hold,
Grabbed his arm, each then reaching for buoyancy, to be bold,
Found in the form of a large piece of debris, no need to be told,
An upturned barrel quickly filling with water, as though to scold.

They then grabbed hold of a chest, a foot locker with trapped air,
Offering to provide sufficient support, in this, their great despair,
It enabled them to make their way towards the rocky platform,
Which was within view below the cracking brilliance of the storm.

Piercing light was delivered, another lightning strike from stem,
Different shades of darkness outlining the scene before them,
A sudden burst of energy within them peaked their ability,
Where did the effort come from, this splurge of activity.

Within as little as half a minute they found themselves so near,
So near the edge of the platform that encompassed their fear,
The platform was covered in crashing waves and ebbing surf,
A giant cauldron at the boil, which was to become their berth.

Without warning a tidal surge of water lifted them both,
Up and over a jagged lip, over the mass of water's froth,
A miraculous salvation from harm for which they were grateful,
Tossed like a cork in a barrel after being so careful.

"Quickly! Willem; to me; grab my hand!" yelled Pieter so loud,
His voice penetrating the cold of the night, the darkest, the shroud,
Where the wind and spray from the ocean stung at their faces,
So unprotected they were, here at the worst of places.

Willem reached for Pieter, stretching beyond his doubt,
Until fingertip touched fingertip, their hands gripping about,
Now clasped together like welded metal, a single cast of iron,
Courage hence instilled within each, each now with heart of lion.

Pieter pulled Willem to, amidst the fury of gut-wrenching surges,
At the platform, made visible now and again, the surf edges,
In and out, undulating and fierce, ocean and rock, the thunder,
They scrambled now to a temporary safe haven behind a boulder.

The ocean continued to smash up and around,
Tearing at all in its way, upon all of the ground,
Followed by a freak wave of enormous size,
Encasing them in terror, of mortality to prise.

The lone man and boy gasped for air as the water ebbed back,
Easing off a little from its most heinous attack,
But the fury of the ocean was preparing for another assault,
The beat and bash, man, ship and rock, never to halt.

Pieter looked up and saw his opportunity for salvation,
A rampart of sorts, a mass of crumbling rock, gifting levitation,
Detritus in all its glory made for a steep but passable way out,
A clear way to the summit of the cliff face before them so stout.

Rock, stone and boulders had fallen away from the cliff,
Its true height obscured by dark of night, the ocean and its riff,
No sound heard from above, no sight of anything familiar,
No tree, only sound and sea, that cliff: in life nothing similar.

The height of the cliff, in fact, did obscure,
Did take from mind what was natural and pure,
Inaccuracy of perception provided the mind,
The insufficient light, it all did bind.

"Willem; with me; come with me, NOW," ordered the tall man,
Together they scrambled up gradient of detritus, this their plan,
Losing two steps from every three in their rush,
To secure safe haven, ever on, to push and push.

Each slipped numerous times, too many to count,
Fingernails splintered, blood soaked, pain did mount,
Much pain and caked in mud, they climbed higher and higher,
Ignoring abrasions and torn muscles, they seek their desire.

Every part of the body was a machine set to automatic,
Their every tissue that binds them working so frantic,
Ligaments and mind: both physical and mental: sheer panic,
No thought but of survival, they were berserk, crazed... manic.

Salvation wasn't too far ahead, they could see and feel it,
Looking up momentarily to see what was ahead, so close to spit,
But the light of night caused false crest to fill their vision,
They pushed on, evermore, shaking from mind this visual treason.

How much further did they need to drive,
In order for life to be secured, to thrive,
How long until victory was won,
This sheer misery, opposite to fun.

But reach the top they did, just as a little cloud moved aside,
Then disappeared and came, cloud racing, to ride and ride,
But they caught glimpse from atop the cliff on which they stood,
Exhausted but forced to endure, to watch below the great flood.

HOLLANDIA NOVA, 1712

The Zuytdorp was in three pieces, thrashed and torn,
A few bodies barely seen, to sight a thorn,
And together the boy and man collapsed, their minds in a knot,
Upon the edge of the cliff, 115 feet high, there on the spot.

But conscious they were as they gasped for air,
From where they lay they could only stare,
A wave of relief empowering both to sit up and look,
Opened mouthed and in disbelief, Poseidon an evil crook.

Shock had momentary hold on their conscience,
Before clearly, a surge of adrenalin, not a science,
The natural bodies defence to protect and to serve,
They embraced the return of sanity, and feeling to nerve.

For now, out of exhilaration,
No adrenalin from action,
Torment of mind had returned,
Pain of injury now quickly learned.

Little by little it was all taken in,
Information deciphered, so thick, not thin,
The entire scene of destruction,
Cargo cast far and wide.

Barrels crashing against rocky platform,
Everything that moved was a weapon amidst this storm,
If anyone was alive then they required good prayer,
That was all they could do, this odd looking pair.

They could do nought of this situation,
Hands bound tight: to complete inaction,
These two skeletons of humanity, drawn to face their reality,
Now starved upon course, their voyage of obscurity.

Tired from the escape of sinking ship,
Tired from the fight across the cliff's lip,
Tired from the climb to higher station,
Completely exhausted beyond all imagination.

Guilty for doing nothing for possible survivors below,
The breaking of human conditioning, to sea, to throw,
Guilty of being alive whilst many others were now dead,
The laying of souls, never to rest in this wet tomb, their bed.

A few bodies could be seen, dashed against rocks,
In teasing action, as though the devil happily mocks,
But a silhouette falls before the surging of wave,
Cast upon them both now a vision from the grave.

"HEY, up here; we're up here!" shouted Willem as he waved,
His arms an invitation, most frantic, for company they craved,
But the vision was apparition, not true at all, nothing real,
The light and storm playing upon him, to savagely deal.

The stinging of rain upon his face was numbing,
His eyes betraying, and below the waves thrashing,
Pieter made Willem lower his hand, grabbing gently his wrist,
Wishing him to hold the pointless aid, to refrain and desist.

HOLLANDIA NOVA, 1712

"Save yourself, Willem," said Pieter, eyes sincere and mellow,
Looking upon the boy of fourteen: a boy, this young fellow,
The boy returned the gaze, eyes momentarily tied by knot,
"They can't see nor hear you," the statement truer than not.

"Are we to do nothing at all, just sit here amidst the slaughter?"
"Avert your eyes, Willem. That's all you can do," advised Pieter,
"But I must do something to help," Willem replied,
Pieter realizing this minute that 'man' tag should be applied.

"Then do as I do, Willem. Keep your eyes open this night,
Ignore the pain you see; ignore the horrors, ignore the fright,
Watch, Willem; watch with your entire might,
Maintain a vision of where people lay until first light."

"Keep a note on where they may be found on the break day,
For us to venture down, pull all ashore, to soil safely lay,
We may find survivors, Willem, but we must focus,
We must hold our nerve, be the bull, be the Taurus."

"Harvest the fruits of our labour,
Keep all in our favour,
Set ourselves to task,
This is all that I ask."

Willem nodded acceptance of the task set before him,
Both casting their eyes upon the horrors of the shipwreck so grim,
The developing scene, a betrayal cast down from heaven above,
Willem thought: how could God do this to those he did love.

Quite rapidly now the cold of the storm penetrated deep,
Willem began to shiver, there upon the cliff so steep,
For the panic which had overridden the effect of the cold,
Had now dissipated, no defence hence scored, none to hold.

"Here, Willem," said Pieter. "Sit in front of me and keep warm,
between my legs sit tight, we must try and ignore the storm."
Pieter looked round, into the dark and saw nothing behind,
Infrequent exposures, open land, no good cover brought to mind.

"I see nothing," continued Pieter. "Nothing but open ground."
Willem was now seated in front of the man, some comfort found,
"Remain strong; stay as warm as possible, remain untainted,
Stay as strong as can be until the storm has abated."

"From our experiences on ship I think I can safely surmise,
That this cold is not common, but an unfortunate surprise."
"I've heard many stories," said Willem as his teeth chattered,
His body convulsed a little with shudders of pain that mattered.

"That this land is as cold in winter months, to encase and smother,
As it is hot, when the sun is at its fiercest, during the summer."
"No one has been around long enough to tell the difference,"
Voiced Pieter above the storm that continued its deliverance.

"This job of ours will be a hard one," added Pieter, "I was wrong,
I don't think we should remain aloft the wreck for too long,
I feel the pain of this bitter cold within me,
As I know you feel it within you, for I can see."

HOLLANDIA NOVA, 1712

Willem was a shivering wreck, tooth and nail,
Pieter looked again, far from mind the throwing of towel,
"Willem; I don't think we'll find good shelter, but we must try,
A hollow, something sturdy to protect, on something to rely."

Without a further word the two stood up and proceeded away,
Stooped low with backs to storm they searched for place to stay,
Away from the cliff, away from the dismay,
In search for a haven and from which to pray.

It wasn't long before they came across a small re-entrant,
A small stream with banks of little concern but not pleasant,
They followed this a short distance before coming upon scrub,
Thick and impenetrable, upon their arms to severely rub.

"Maybe we should turn back," said Willem with growing concern,
"Up here, Willem. I see several boulders. Follow me, to stern."
They stepped from the low ground, halting beside large boulders,
Settled behind these as the wind hampered their weary shoulders.

Away from the blast of the wind and the soaking of rain,
Sought shelter for the remainder of the night, away from the pain,
Curled up and holding each other close, their misery to bury,
But could not sleep whilst the storm continued with its fury.

In the least they gathered rest, better than nothing at all,
Some semblance of energy restored, not all to stall,
Wanting to live on and to provide aid in the morning,
Thoughts on possible survivors, something on which to cling.

In time the storm did blow itself clear of the coast,
The sun was almost upon them, a warm and welcome host,
But currently it was time for some sleep,
Which fell easily upon them, and they in one heap.

LEADERSHIP

Birdsong was filling the air, birds from some distance away,
A melody of choruses that seemed unperturbed by the night's fray,
The sound rather mellow and pleasant, so sweet,
As two fragile forms awoke to the morning, the light to greet.

There was a bite of cold of the air, not a cloud in the sky,
The sun having broken the horizon, now quite high,
But the cold had less effect upon them than the night before,
When they were drenched to the bone, much misery to score.

Their clothing was torn and a little shredded,
A layer of protection gone, sure to be dreaded,
A little wet from the ocean and rain,
Suffering from bruises and a little pain.

Willem was the first to sit up, followed by Pieter, sound heard,
Both shivering as they opened their eyelids, now stirred,
And the vibration hit them both, resonant echoing, unfamiliar,
A long way off, a penetrating sound, mystifying but clear.

"Did you hear that, Pieter?" asked Willem, sound eerie but sweet,
"I did, Willem," the man answered as he stood up upon his feet,
Each looking out towards the north-east, each to broach,
From where the sound made its unwavering approach.

"And I think I know what it is," on instinct he relies,
"What?" asked Willem as he looked up into Pieter's eyes,
Willem saw the reflection of humanity, alive in the sodden body,
Scratches and bruises covering his arms and face, looking shoddy.

Clothes torn and tattered, his trousers ripped down one entire side,
Baring the flesh of his leg to the world, nowhere to hide,
His shoes missing and socks soaked with blood,
Patches of varying colour, covered by wet and dry mud.

"I think it's the men of this world, the owners of soil, this turf."
"Wretched souls," replied Willem, casting his eyes upon the earth,
Pieter corrected: "There has been much talk; much hearsay."
"Do you think they'll eat us this day?"

A false smile caressed Pieter's face, "No. But let's forget that,
Forget it for the minute, we are nothing on which to grow fat,
We must get back to the cliff, view the damage,
Find survivors if we can, if survive any did manage."

Leading the way back to the cliff face, Pieter looked behind,
Ensured that Willem was close by and at hand, kept on mind,
And before they knew it they were stepping up towards the ledge,
From atop the cliff , looking down, making silent pledge.

Such a site could never be explained; their feelings of despair,
Their depression, the horror of seeing bodies lying everywhere,
There upon the now exposed platform of rock, the ocean so mild,
And yet the night before it was so untamed and severely wild.

HOLLANDIA NOVA, 1712

There was debris everywhere, not a single foot of ground bare,
Every part of the Zuytdorp now a wreck, dolour on which to stare,
Crates, barrels, cannons, cloth and sacks: all of these things,
Every single item of commerce was free of its holdings.

Everything splashed upon the scene as though in reckless doubt,
All former glory gone, the ship torn into three, losing the bout,
Losing the bout!! There was no coming back: a sheer misery,
When suddenly a voice leapt up from behind them, a victory.

"Pieter, is that you?" asked a weary voice,
A man we know, Ariaen Leyden; oh, rejoice,
Pieter and Willem turned to this presence,
Half startled to death by the broken silence.

"My God," shouted an exuberant Pieter. "We thrive, we thrive,
Ariaen; thank God... oh my… you're alive, you're alive."
 He stepped towards the man of 28 years, a man of the sea,
Such a sight for sore eyes, it filled him with such glee.

Ariaen, a common sailor who had made many voyages to Batavia,
Three occasions, perchance, much experience held, now a savour,
He'd travelled between the countries of Asia for some time now,
Under the keep of the VOC: he quit the sea, he would never allow.

"I'm well," was all he could muster, no formal trope,
And from behind the man came further hope,
A mass of people, twelve all told, each as weathered as the first,
Dressed as lepers, in rags, but still they quenched Pieter's thirst.

And a majority were without footwear upon their feet,
Feet that had been lacerated by rocks, so harshly beat,
Some of those present were in shock, were soaking wet,
Cold all the night, from the early winter's storm already met.

"How many are there of you?" asked Pieter, pessimism cured,
"We're seventeen, including me, but four of them are injured."
"What kind of injuries?" asked Pieter wishing to hear more,
As those behind Ariaen closed the gap, looking bleak and poor.

Sunken faces worn by them all, seemingly gone, life's desire,
Like the embers disappear from the remnants of a blazing fire,
Life gone from their eyes, stripped bear of strength and power,
Nothing on which to gift praise, no gift in which to shower.

But they were alive and that it something better than nought,
What more could one ask, what more could be truly sought,
"Broken bones, mostly; and most of the walking, are whipped,
Cuts and abrasions in large number, skin in places so stripped."

Pieter looked upon Ariaen and saw a gash on his forehead,
A deep wound that had clearly removed some bone, easily read,
All had some form of injury, large and small. "You too are hurt,
We need cleaning materials, good cloth, any raggedy old shirt."

"It appears so. It hurts like hell to tell you the truth, a bother,
But there is more suffering here today than I can ever suffer."
"We need to move down to the wreck," started Pieter by choice,
Before looking upon the others and raising his voice.

"To look for survivors; others that may be trapped,
Who may require our assistance, well and truly sapped."
"No, Pieter," said Ariaen. "We've been dover the wreck already,
Two other men and I, but it is hard down there, far too unsteady."

"We've searched everywhere and not another soul has survived."
"Are you sure...? Maybe you missed someone; someone alive,
We can give hope; hope remaining for some unfortunate soul,
Someone stranded below this cliff, in this heinous, concave bowl."

Ariaen grabbed his friend upon the upper arms amidst stare,
"No, Pieter. We've tried. There is no one to be found there."
"Then what's to be done; what can we do?
For I refuse to believe it is all through."

"Supplies… we also need a firm shelter… maybe some wood,
Bandages and medicine for the sick would be immensely good,
We need tools for the cutting splints, but we need water the most,
Some food… anything to survive this place, our new host."

"And a cannon," voiced Cornelis Lieffers from behind,
A seaman of 19 years, of vast experience, but of poor mind,
"To signal a passing ship,
To aid is securing a return trip."

"Shoes," voiced another further back, "we also need shoes."
Pieter looked down at the man's feet, poor condition, old news,
Yes, indeed, there was much to be sought, much to secure,
Anything for their sanity; anything to keep them morally pure.

For it would be easy to go insane here,
To ridicule and pass on poor sneer,
To spite another for no good reason,
Upon land to cause treason.

Pieter looked at them all, saw a similarity: they were each a lamb,
Like babies in crib being tended, infants being rocked in a pram,
Freely admitting, flocking around a single soul,
It seemed that Ariaen had adopted the leadership role.

But Pieter felt that he had more to offer these people so near,
Each a soul to be catered for, each owed a life quite dear,
"I'm Pieter, I aided the administration by tending the rations,
I have exercised my ambition and expertise upon many stations."

"Upon land and the sea, I have laid visit to many ports,
All before I was nine and twenty, accurate in all of my reports,
I soon decided upon the comfort of dry land, both honest and fair,
And grew to change once more and decided to work elsewhere."

"I have many degrees and sound knowledge on navigation,
I maintain sound mind and ambition, high regard for civilization,
It would honour me if you'd all allow me the opportunity,
To help in this predicament of ours, for short stay or perpetuity."

A man took a few steps forward, those around him stirred,
"I am Hendrik Blaauw. Ariaen knows me, so I am assured,
I am seven and forty, have spent my life upon the sea so blue,
Why should the task of command and rescue go to one as you?"

HOLLANDIA NOVA, 1712

Pieter opened his mouth, to attend further rhetoric, "I have—",
"Yes, yes; you have degrees," Hendrik replied, in effort to save,
Save good position by applying sarcastically, instilled hate,
Hoping all those, here and now, would take the bait.

He turned to look at the others around,
Could see all eyes upon him, interest found,
"Does common paper hold more authority than experience?
I have worked skin to bone, I am tempered, have much patience."

"I am simply offering my hand," said Pieter in defence,
"It's for you to decide what to make of my good essence."
"Well I say that we make of it right now," Hendrik said to tote,
"Who shall be in command of this shipwrecked crew? Let's vote!"

"Aye!" shouted one; "here, here," came another; and one there,
"All of those in favour of me, place your hands up in the air,"
Commanded Hendrik, pushing his own hand up in desperation,
And eight hands showed themselves after a little hesitation.

"The tally has spoken," said Hendrik. "Seven votes, and mine,
That makes a grand total of eight,
The other six will be yours,
Which makes a tally of seven, if you put up your paws."

And Pieter was pleased to see that Willem had voted for him,
It filled him with much pleasure, full to the brim,
"Wait! What of the lame, those that are injured and not here?"
Asked Ariaen in defence of his trusted friend, the votes to steer.

"Don't they have a vote?" pushed Ariaen, forcing the play,
"I have many years at sea and know, gangrene will have its say,"
Said Hendrik. "It will visit them each, and of this take note,
That a dead man cannot be relied upon to make a vote."

"And what of me?" stated Ariaen, "I have changed my mind,
I wish to make a stand. I'm of higher station and kind."
"There's no rank here," came a voice from the back,
A straight forward assault, a plain attack.

"That's right," confirmed Hendrik. "We're no longer on the sea,
Our survival depends on us living off the land, with you I plea,
Think hard on this, don't throw your vote away, we are so few,
I shall serve you all until a ship comes to our rescue."

"Which won't be long now," said Ariaen to all those listening,
Listening to the argument unfold as the sun sat glistening,
"I know that the Kockenge will be off these shores soon....
within the week for sure, whether by day or by light of moon."

"When we were at Table Bay I heard of others whilst on deck,
We can expect such ships as the Oostersteyn, the Zuyderbeeck,
The Belvliet, Popkensburg; the Corsloot,
And even the good ship Oude Zyp to boot."

"All to come this way over the next month, as soon as next week,
Not all will be seen; not all will come within range as we shriek,
Calling them to us with waving arms will do no good,
We need to build a signal fire and ply it with dry wood."

"For immediate ignition will be required when the time is right,
And we need to get a cannon," added Ariaen with eyes so bright,
They then falling upon Cornelis Lieffers, it was his idea,
An idea to save them all with cannon fire, a true seer.

"We must bury the dead and collect rations where possible,
And much, much more to come, but we are strong and able."
"Here, here," yelled Dirck Fret from the rear. "Let's be fair,
All those that vote for Ariaen put your hand in the air."

And to the astonishment of Hendrik a show of nine hands appear,
Each held high, including Willem and Pieter, who stood near,
"Not counting the soon-to-be-dead," added Pieter to the insult,
Extremely excited and overcome by the massive result.

"So as it is spoken, let it be done," said Hendrik in defeat,
The evil in his eyes brewing something behind mask, a sheet,
For it all sounded like a conspiracy against him and out of form,
He tried ignoring the comment against those injured by the storm.

SALVAGE AND SALVES

The storm had done its job well,
The pounding surf and the swell,
All having smashed the hull of the ship,
Driven it into shallow water, to tear and rip.

In watery grave,
And now gentle wave,
Two to ten feet deep, surrounded by water on all sides, this wreck,
Beside the shoreline platform, inside out, an unrecognizable deck.

Easy to see how many reached safety, only wishing it were more,
Tangled rigging alongside a fallen mast connecting ship to shore,
Precariously unstable, not to remain long where it currently lay,
It was a devastating site, beyond belief, faces now soberly grey.

A cliff of limestone [around 90 feet high at the actual wreck site],
At the foot a mass of jagged edges and boulders to spite,
Sharp-edged rocks and little sand of which to speak,
Stretching 65 feet wide, and 6.5 above sea level at low peak.

To all of those now looking upon the scene, seeing far and wide,
From the cliff, along the entire coast [for 155 miles] to either side,
An unbroken stretch of cliff disappeared into the horizon,
So daunting to say the least, but also beautiful beyond reason.

HOLLANDIA NOVA, 1712

A carpet of silver could be seen far below, shimmering bright,
Glimmering in patches, here and there, in the morning's light,
Every chest broken, treasure inside revealed from behind shield,
The biggest decision was where to start, of their lives to rebuild.

Ariaen said: "We need to be systematic about our salvage,"
Looking at the others: "I see the wonder in eyes so savage,
The glittering of the silver below lighting up your eyes,
Listen to me, money is worthless if you're dead, I tell no lies."

"It'll all still be there next week and the week after that,
Help yourself if you wish but remember one thing flat,
What you salvage belongs to the VOC and will be taken back,
You'll receive no special favour, so of scruples don't lack."

"Some of you need shoes; that is a priority most worthy,
We need wood for shelter, if possible a cannon most sturdy,
Just the one will serve our purpose, if we can manage its weight,
But basic needs must be sought, choose wisely of this freight."

"A working breech block will help the most for the cannon's need,
Food and fresh water, and above all something on which to feed,
Barrels for storage, and anything else you think appropriate,
Anything not tied down, think clearly of plan, don't deviate."

"This is the calm after the storm, you need to all be bold,
For none of us truly knows what the future may hold,
We may not get another opportunity to gather our supply,
So let us make the most of it, on one and all our lives rely."

Ariaen then waved his hand frantically about, his face a stage,
Trying with great effort to release himself of bondage and rage,
For a fly did ingratiate itself upon him, even in June, winter,
Thanks to low temperatures, there being but a single flesh eater.

There were nods of agreement and the men went to work,
Climbing down towards the wreck, their life-giving stork,
Slipping upon the steep bank as they made for what remained,
Of the good ship Zuytdorp, another name the ocean had claimed.

Little was said during the task, the feeling of dread,
Clothing sought and shoes being pulled from the dead,
Bodies collected and moved towards the cliff, there to lay,
To hopefully be pulled to drier land, for men on which to pray.

For the need of man was a funeral and last words,
To seek eternal life, spirits on the wind, like birds,
For the sanctity of heaven and the bliss of afterlife,
To forsaken the natural life and all its strife.

But more still, no need for the corpses to rot and cause disease,
For horrendous smell to waft up to survivors, to mercilessly tease,
And if the ship was to be visited in the near future,
To visit unrestricted by unpleasant scene would be there pleasure.

There was no doubt of mind that visits would need to be made,
But confidence needed to be instilled, no need to be afraid,
And reminders of death was a curse upon itself, this we know,
Besides, the dead deserved burial, to keep spirits high, not low.

HOLLANDIA NOVA, 1712

Several men tried to get one of the smaller bronze swivel guns,
Drag it ashore with breech block, and visit cabin, the boson's,
Rope needed to haul the large and heavy mass up cliff,
Surely something of desire and need, even a skiff.

So much to consider, so much on which to think,
Act fast but methodically, for the ship may drift and sink,
A tide to drag the remains of wreck far out to sea,
What would they do then, what would their predicament be?

Swivels were mounted on the poop, the highest part of the ship,
Currently quite accessible, but watch your footing, don't slip,
Several breech blocks were taken ashore in the end,
But swivel guns far too heavy, no way, of this, to amend.

Breech blocks were 12-18 inches long, weighed 28 pounds each,
Easier to portage if only they'd wrecked upon a beach,
And a pair of callipers and brass dividers scored, for navigation,
If later they should decide to build a boat, to avoid deprivation.

But for the most they searched for water and food,
Even Willem was much in the mood,
Everyone able was seen there, scampering about,
Looking and searching for salvage, of congratulations to shout.

Willem then fell upon an areas abundant in wealth,
Not entirely sure as to what they were called, here upon a shelf,
An area encrusted with... were they oysters, abalone, periwinkles?
Whelks, mussels and other shellfish, possibly rock barnacles.

Could they survive solely upon shellfish and nothing more,
How long would such commodity last, this limited store,
Willem was too young to consider the facts of survival,
Wishing and praying for another ship, for its safe arrival.

How long would any ship supply last all of those alive,
In the face of the impending difficulty where disease could thrive,
For there was a few on the brink of gangrene and death,
Lives on the edge of a sword, ready to draw last breath.

One of the searchers found dry powder for musket, but no musket,
Another a possible banquet, but found instead an empty basket,
A great stash of tobacco tins, but contents and lids missing,
Some broken bottles of brandy, not worthy of assessing.

The dislodged figurehead of a pregnant women made of wood,
From the Zuytdorp, thrown against rocks, it once proudly stood,
Now carried into a cavern below the cliff face for safe keeping,
A memory of the past, for their humanity is their thinking.

Far too large to carry to the top at present,
Maybe later, when time could be spent,
A memento of past life, a flag to recall,
A memorial of some description, strong meaning to all.

The figure was from the stern of the ship, a figure of passion,
She had a small plump face and bore a placid expression,
She was the only woman amongst them, none other to speak,
Carved of wood, not flesh, a prize worth saving, one to keep.

HOLLANDIA NOVA, 1712

One by one, in there two's and three's,
Men appeared briefly upon the cliff top, their on their knees,
Placing down their salvage most gently as though baby to bed,
Before returning to the work, bodies wearily, but onwards lead.

And the bodies of the dead were collected below,
Accumulated on the platform, there to stow,
Stacked precariously, shoes taken by those that wore them,
Brief prayer to accompany their removal, the item a gem.

The ship's sails were torn apart – what was left – but taken,
Would be employed well as a shelter, to life a token,
And sheets or blankets for the bandaging of broken limbs,
For future breaks, of fingers and feet, and other things.

All men were different, in some large or small way,
And some here wished to doctor, to help where they may,
To give that gift of giving, to help where best they could,
Not knowing in some cases whether or not they should.

The collection of dead was the worst, a most horrid sight,
Silent and frantic calls reaching for the sky now bright,
But fight on they did against every normal sense,
Do all they could for dignity, sparing no expense.

And then a trove found like no other,
Like the breast milk for baby from mother,
Green bottle of alcohol for some men so weak,
Square in shape, filled with gin, some solace to seek.

Some of the more fragile-of-mind did hide poor intention,
Sought to carry many bottles off to hide in hidden station,
Somewhere upon the cliff face overlooking the sea, their store,
For drunkenness to pitch and play, to alcohol a whore.

Here sat Gerrit Jongbloet, Jacob Albertsz, and friend,
Jacobus Nuyts and Cornelius Brouwer, their sanity to amend,
They had wondered from duty not long after it did commence,
Drawing their bottles close into their chests, ready to dispense.

Wrapping their arms around the neck of a bottle,
To pour and pour, to throttle and throttle,
Caressing them as though they were wives of advantage,
Sucking the bottles dry, their moral sanctity in a rage.

Weaning the glass bottles of every drop,
Not knowing when, or if ever, they would stop,
Becoming drunk and loud amidst the misfortune so fallen,
Fallen upon them all, appetites so horribly swollen.

The four men with broken limbs lay not so far to one side,
Clutching their ears to prevent the awful sound, this tide,
Such drunken slander, so horrid, of their scruples it did tear,
And screams were emitted by those with breaks, unable to bear.

Dirck Fret, 35; and 29 year old Wiebbe Leuftink, sailors,
Had turned to doctoring, upon the needy great favours,
The strain of their task being very real and unparalleled,
At their wits end, their patience and anger just swelled.

HOLLANDIA NOVA, 1712

Never before had either of them provided medical assistance,
And with no one of sufficient knowledge, was this a penance,
But for what they achieved the victims were most grateful,
And the drunken swine so close were unhelpful and hateful.

No one deserved this mockery, this absence,
An absence of morals and good temperance,
This drunkenness was beyond belief,
Did nothing to alleviate suffering or give relief.

The two good men, Dirck and Wiebbe, could do little,
As the drunks suckled upon their bottles amidst spittle,
Their passion for the green bottle, their precious gin,
Only aiding the weak in committing an audacious sin.

But the gin was a small saviour as well,
Given to the sick in small amounts, in pores to gel,
Was a passion which would help take the pain away,
To help those poor souls where upon the ground they lay.

Francisco Roelofsz had a broken leg and a punctured gut wound,
Seemingly forever on the edge of consciousness he swooned,
Johannes Snitquer a broken arm and fractured skull,
Constantly, forever, silent and still, in staring but full lull.

Marinus Leynsen had a broken arm and several broken ribs,
Fought hard to breath, on life he held but small dibs,
And Hayman Jorisz, of unsound mind, had two broken legs,
A poor condition, unlikely to ever walk again, for savour he begs.

Dirck looked to Wiebbe as the noise from the drunks drifted down,
Falling upon the shelter for wounded, they displaying a frown,
Several planks of wood and sail cloth melded as one,
A shelter from possible rain and the glimmering sun.

It wasn't the grandest attempt anyone had made at pitching,
Not a great architectural feat of hitching and stitching,
But for the time they'd been allowed they fared reasonably well,
Providing a little comfort, if any, from conditions a spell.

Out of earshot, Dirck said to Wiebbe, "I fear for Hayman,
That he won't last the week, and I am no worthy layman."
"Hmmm," acknowledged Wiebbe. "I fear for Francisco, he sinks,
I'll go and see Ariaen, ask him what he thinks."

"Don't give him too much credit, Wiebbe. He's just a man like us,
Do not provide him too much fuss,
Refrain from giving too much satisfaction,
It will go to his head, this granting of position."

"If it proves too much for him, if he fails to jump through hoop,
Then will be the time to change the leadership of this group,"
Said Wiebbe as he moved off without further word from Dirck,
Both good and clear-thinking men, of work never to shirk.

Dirck pulled a piece of cloth from a damaged bucket ,
Wiped the perspiration from Johannes' forehead, to pet,
The bruising upon his skull being very evident,
A large swelling and mostly red and a concave dent.

HOLLANDIA NOVA, 1712

There was much pressure beneath the skull,
Seemingly pale, this flesh of man, this hull,
And the worst was feared for his well-being,
His fever was very strong amidst light mewling.

REMARKABLE FAUNA

Wiebbe approached Ariaen who had just appeared at the lip,
Above the cliff carrying one end of a plank, from broken ship,
Willem coming up from the rear, proving himself to be worthy,
Together they placed the plank down, tired, slow, and both filthy.

Willem was excited within, wishing to prove himself a man,
So patiently he worked, fulfilling his duty, a boy with a plan,
Lifting now, one end of the plank, and pulled it with great effort,
Over to a pile that he had growing rather large, bulky and stout.

"The boy works well," noted Wiebbe, smiling at the boy,
And waving away a single fly as it came in to annoy,
"He's a man now," said Ariaen, seeing Willem's mouth erupt,
Erupt into a smile, such a comment could never corrupt.

Wiebbe reflected briefly on the boy before making announcement,
For his reason of errand, of his anxieties which did ferment,
"The wounded are in a bad way... the gin did work well,
But won't last the whole night, and so gone our protective shell."

"There'll be much suffering later tonight,
But pain to be suffered before first light."
It was easy to see how genuinely concerned he was for all,
How strong in morals he was, how he held himself, lofty and tall.

HOLLANDIA NOVA, 1712

Pieter there too, behind with sack, from work both sore and stiff,
Asked he: "What about those drunken bums over near the cliff?
Can't we seize the bottles they have, give them to those in need,
Prevent this absorbent waste, this tireless greed?"

Wiebbe added: "Oh, they have more than you think, that's no lie,
They've taken a great quantity of bottles, have them close by,
They've hidden them mostly, but maintain a few by their side,
They're settled in for a long and drunken ride."

"Take them by force," said Pieter, "do not be kind, don't woo."
"They have knives..." commenced Wiebbe. "What can I do?
What is it to us that they choose to crawl inside a bottle; really?
If that is their wont, their love, then let them hold them dearly."

"Inflicted by the devil. It will be to their own demise," Pieter said,
"We need the gin: can we take them when they go to bed?"
Ariaen commented then: "But if they don't sleep or stray…"
Said Peter: "We think. What is it that we can do for you anyway?"

"The wounded, as I have said; they're all in a bad way,
But some more than others, for them all I sincerely pray,
Most of us have something to remember the storm by,
But those four... I think time is short. Death, for them, does vie."

"Francisco has a broken leg as well as a punctured gut,
We can't do anything for the wound, no scalpel to cut,
Nothing to do except bandage it and hope for the best,
Endeavour to do all we can and provide them with much rest."

"Nevertheless, the wound will infect, unless we clean and close,
It's going to turn gangrene, and before we know it, on the nose."
"Can we attain anything from the ship's doctor, from his cabin?"
Asked Pieter of Ariaen, "Somehow maintain an uplift of chin."

"His cabin isn't far from the skipper's. Pieter, you were in there,
What was it like? Did you see supplies, or was it laid bare?"
"Last night it was like hell; this morning I conducted a search,
Of company or personal belongings... nothing but unsteady lurch.

"Even now the ship is wavering a little: a small wave hit the side,
But I continued on, knowing we are short on time, I did abide,
Most of the quarters are below the surface, a sheer hazard,
I prepared myself for the worst, of myself I did gird."

"But the cabinet in which the medicine is kept has been spoilt,
As much by the storm itself and also the waters of salt,
Everything will be ruined, for the ocean and rocks give no favour,
Gone all the goodness, smell and flavour, nought there to savour."

Asked Wiebbe: "Isn't it worth another try?
Something may be found, this you cannot deny."
"I'll have another look," volunteered Pieter, not confident at all,
Feeling no confidence in this effort, as though on errand, a fool.

And he was correct, for in the end nothing could be salvaged,
Neither doctor's belongings or medicine, all had been ravaged,
Said Ariaen: "Meanwhile we must provide them comfort."
Concluded Wiebbe: "I'll return to my station, increase my effort."

Another did then appear at the cliff, a scenery of sea and sound,
A regular seaman as could ever be found,
Jan Wysvliet put down a bucket: [his coming end due to denial],
Willem came in from the side and moved it to his stockpile.

"Jan, can I ask something of you?" queried Ariaen quite calm,
"Certainly. What is it?" Jan, easily lead astray: to hold in palm,
"Take another man with you and find a campsite,
Not too far away from the cliff; somewhere... just right."

"...but far enough to be away from the drunks over by the cliff,
They are just over there: drunken state and gin, easy to whiff."
"Sure," acknowledged Jan, tired reflection showing, easy to see,
As well as in the way he held himself. "I'll take Harmen with me."

Harmen Akkerman and Jan pushed on into the unknown,
Ready for anything, in their direction, to be thrown,
To a site where the Indian Ocean could be seen both far and wide,
And having quickly established a site for a camp they set to stride.

They decided to continue with a reconnaissance, to be gratified,
For it wasn't enough for these two men to be easily satisfied,
Men of the sea looking for adventure, for something to be met,
Not content with such a small accomplishment as previously set.

They commenced upon their reconnaissance of the area with glee,
Towards where the sound did seemingly grow, wishing to see,
The sweet call falling upon the light breeze and flowing their way,
The same one heard by Pieter and themselves, earlier that day.

From the edge of the cliff inwards for about 1,300 feet was void,
Nothing except a little low heath vegetation, solitude enjoyed,
Beyond that there existed very dense scrub for two miles,
Tea-tree and eucalyptus, a place favourable to criminal exiles.

The trees themselves well spaced, able to provide opportunity,
Ample enough for the making of raft or shelter, to avoid ferity,
To lease life more opportunity and saviour, that grand prize,
All was here for the taking should the need arise.

As it was, however, there was plenty of salvage from the wreck,
Enough to currently serve all of their purposes, keep life in check,
Which included material for the making of wild and blazing fires,
That is, once planks had dried, hence suited for their desires.

The going was tough on the men for they were already exhausted,
Tired from the salvage operation and not sufficiently rested,
Not to mention that they had gone without food passing their lips,
Since that day when sunk: forgone memory of salted bacon strips.

The sky was a beautiful blue and there was not a cloud to be seen,
Both knew winter was approaching, of this they were not keen,
And the clear sky so high above would soon be gone,
Winter storms and sullies, so close this future, not long.

Several gullies were present amidst a little undulating ground,
Each several hundred feet apart, small ridges and mound,
Each stretching out from the land and towards the coast,
Some being quite deep, a savage land, an unpleasant host.

HOLLANDIA NOVA, 1712

Like small streams during winter after heavy rain,
But dry for the remainder of the year, underfoot a pain,
Harmen and Jan knelt down to drew handfuls of fresh water,
A small trickling from the night's storm, of dryness to alter.

Small rock holes were also found to hold up to 12 gallons or more,
Although an unreliable source of water, of requirements no bore,
Collection was the key, storage to become desire and need,
And next on the agenda was a source on which to feed.

Further inland there was a great expanse of undulating sandplain,
Stunted with low scrub, sheer desert by appearance, carpet so lain,
Like an ocean dotted with acacias, eucalypts, banksias and other,
To these men of the open sea, this was enough to smother.

Vastly different than the sights and smells of home and glory,
A land bound by cities at their fullest, amidst talk and story,
The scene before them was devastating to say the least,
This carpet of mystery, this awakening of unseen beast.

The heat of afternoon built up, dwarfing the cold from night,
And so, as it does at sea on long voyages, it played its delight,
Their feet started swelling up with the effort of the walk,
High above a migration of birds, squawking as though to talk.

As they continued on into the clearing, Harmen came to a halt,
"Look, Jan. Over there," said Harmen, pointing, but ready to bolt,
With his head low he tried to aim his finger with great accuracy,
As though it were a weapon, though in palm a vacancy.

"What do you see?" asked Jan as he looked off into the distance,
"A head, I'm sure of it," and so he searched for its reappearance,
"It moved... look... there it is again," Harmen said hurriedly,
"And now it's not moving; it's like a statue," he said quite avidly.

"Ah; yes. I see it too," concurred Jan, withholding a shout,
"It's not moving now. It has great ears and a long snout,
What do you think, for my mind is glassy with fog?"
Concluded Harmen, a satisfaction on self analysis, "A dog."

"No," disagreed Jan, looking upon friend with lowered eyebrows,
Signifying his puzzlement, as such a suggestion allows,
"Look around you, Harmen. This grass is almost chest high,
If it's a dog it'll be the largest dog I've ever seen, I cannot deny."

"It could be standing upon a recent kill, or a dirt mound,
Maybe searching for prey," suggested Harmen. "A great hound."
And then it moved, dashing off as it did leap and bound,
Against the open plains of grass-filled expanse, all around.

A kangaroo as never seen by the eyes of a white man before,
Harmen and Jan cowered in the long grass, afraid evermore,
Now breathless,
Now restless.

Holding their palms to chest, being caught completely by surprise,
The animal moving with such rapid action, small panic did rise,
"Did you see that?" asked Harmen, and then many more,
Fifteen other animals picked up their head, heads galore.

HOLLANDIA NOVA, 1712

Each leaping off as the other had done,
Following the previous, a move to stun,
"My God. I don't believe it. What a sight."
"We must get back, Jan. Bring this to light"

"No, not yet," said Jan, looking at Harmen, within an anxiousness,
"They're just animals, Harmen. We should delve, be witness,
Go beyond where they stood, learn of them, find a weakness,
Clear our heads, learn hard facts, deny our minds this fogginess.

"But not too far, Jan. We don't want to get lost, unsettle the rest."
"Lost," scoffed Jan. "If so then we just head west,
It's as simple as that, but for the minute we must explore,
Come; let's go that way; east; let's look some more."

Before they knew it the day had closed its door,
By which they felt exhausted and fell to the desert floor,
There was no time for a meal of any sort... it had been missed,
The sun disappearing over the horizon: they had hunger to resist.

Their eyes were then drawn to watching that stunning sight,
The appearance of a myriad of colours cast across the starry night,
A great mass of sparkles came out, those made invisible by day,
Providing sufficient light to provide small comfort as they lay.

They lay in the dim light offered by the heavens above,
Being able to see in all directions, a serenity to love,
The cool night comfortable enough to keep them from freezing,
And the sounds of the night reached their ears, it was so amazing.

Huddled together like man and wife helped keep them warm,
Not so hard, gifted by that lack of storm,
It wasn't until the early hours of the morning that they felt cold,
A vacuum of evaporated heat present when they move, to scold.

It was all new to them, completely strange, and sadly,
Too tired from the night before they did sleep soundly,
They slept through the main chorus, the birds and their song,
Music of the morning, of the bush: everything right, not wrong.

And then out of the distance, more serine than first thought,
Sounds of reverberation across the land, that which was sought,
A ceremony taking place upon this strange land: near or far?
A drumming; a sincere acoustic; a fear it did jar.

There could be cannibals,
Maybe wild animals,
Creatures of the unknown,
Something heinous at them thrown.

THE DEVIL IN GIN

The night before Jan and Harmen did sleep,
It was for the others to…. Celebrate, not weep,
But before them now the sun drifting to horizon,
Fine work here, work to remember, to emblazon.

The salvage operation, early morning till dusk, well wrought,
Little undone, they did all they could, or so they thought,
All that could be carried from harm's way conveyed,
That too heavy left till morning, where it lay it stayed.

And before the waves moved in from an abrupt sea,
A shadow fell upon the camp, worries dampening their glee,
For there was still much to do, much to sort, much to consider,
Many resources secured from wreck, much work for the leader.

The prizes unmoved would be going nowhere soon,
With or without high tide, with or without the moon,
Most too heavy to be carried out by smallish waves,
Or taken beneath the surging surf to watery graves.

Some were still attached,
Such as material employed as shield or thatch,
Even if precariously so, most would be available come morning,
In particular the swivel gun, to the deck it had good mooring.

But the bulk of the cheer, their cherished reward for honour,
Was port to cliff under hard sway, under harsh and hard labour,
But so much lost: barrels of wine and beer, the butter, ten sheep,
Rice, bacon and oils; nothing of these to save, to keep.

They were fortunate enough to have rescued some cloth and rope,
Peas, a few plates, many pounds of salted meat, all gave hope,
And vast amounts of meat had been lost to the hungry sea,
So much waste, gone forever, of vast resources now free.

Yes indeed, free they were of all that was home,
To be stranded in this hell, so little known of this biome,
Form measly chunks of bread and anything more lavish,
But they did manage some canvas, this to savour and relish.

That thing needed the least was illness and disease,
But nature was not on their side, not there to appease,
And that required the most, other than medicine was food,
But the salted meat would not last long, their situation no good.

They would make the most of the food whilst it lasted,
And maintain high hope for favourable wind well blasted,
For some source or other to come their way,
For pain of hunger to be held at bay.

The bodies of the dead had been piled on shoreline platform,
Unable to be moved unless hit by very heavy storm,
There they lay, ready to be moved, possibly the next day,
A huge fire and last prayer to send them on their way.

HOLLANDIA NOVA, 1712

Of way we speak, and of this we must be fair,
For not all people are good, of heaven not to share,
Some were destined for place hotter than most,
For man with horns, to forever be their host.

A fire was intended for the deceased all at the same time,
A few words spoken, as best could be offered, some in rhyme,
No honoured guest available but learned men at least,
Someone there, better than none, even if not a priest.

A fire which would not only act as a point from which to cremate ,
But a signal to any coast-passing ship, of their situation to relate,
With the calculations suggested of the ships in port at Table Bay,
It was a reliable guess as to when eyes would easterly lay.

To fall upon them on the horizon, their signal seen,
And the survivors held good reason to remain reasonably keen,
For the Kockenge was expected over the next six or seven days,
Much slower than the Zuytdorp: to come near, to see their blaze.

Meanwhile the four men, drunk and beyond comprehension,
Lay near the edge of the cliff, creating much tension,
Each drowning their sorrows, to where they became oblivious,
Unaware of events amidst their gin, all the fool and treasonous.

A temporary fire had been lit by way of several lamps full of oil,
And a tinderbox procured by Ariaen, held from any great spoil,
Along with a secret maintained by him, a small box of tobacco,
A worthy possession, this and his fire-starter, left to fallow.

But the seamen did uncover the truth of his withholding,
Mostly halfwits, clear lack of intelligence, yet up to deciphering,
They could sum up two and two, possibly not three and three,
Ariaen had little choice and came clean of his tiny *whee*.

The firestarter, his tinderbox, now known by almost all,
But of the little tobacco he held he remained tight lip, to stall,
Stall the sight and smell of his delectable morsel of power,
And now he desired a tree root similar to that of a brier.

Any old tree root would do, in fact,
Something to hollow out, to carry on the act,
The act of puffing and inhaling, nothing near like it,
Forever on his mind was this thing yet made, he did admit.

From time to time,
A scent so sublime,
He sniffed the weed,
A perfume agreed.

Water was then brought to the boil for a dry satchel of tea,
It and a single tumbler rescued from ship of the sea,
Too little for all the survivors, some would miss out,
And a large portion of meat cooked in a pot quite stout.

With plenty enough to fill everyone most contentedly,
The warmth of food in stomach greeted most heartedly,
A small portion of tea would not go wholly missed,
Much more was on the mind, never to be held in fist.

HOLLANDIA NOVA, 1712

The fire was heaven to have and to behold,
Most warily of its dangers, its ability to scold,
But likely wouldn't last, for fuel was low,
Wood needed securing, on fire of which to throw.

They hadn't managed to gather much wood,
That of salvage was, for shelter, reasonably good,
It would be a sin to throw such on fire as it stood,
A roof more apt to appease them as it should.

Even so it was still rather wet from the ocean and storm,
Pieter then made ready to speak and to inform,
For he held a lamp, which he shook to his ear,
And heard nought from within, it was a smallish fear.

That was the last of the oil for all they knew,
The remainder in wreck, or out to ocean as the wind blew,
He stood then with lantern in hand and threw,
Temporarily jolted by anger, by misgivings as they stew.

The injured had been moved closer,
To provide assurance, though they were wiser,
This was their time of need, but not of desire,
For one at least he was ready to retire.

Johannes Snitquer, with the broken arm and fractured skull,
His brain had haemorrhage, and before death the great lull,
Lull of feeling and remorse,
Wishing to live, of course, of course.

And death was like a dream to some,
Clear and understood, no feeling glum,
Some experienced little sorrow, but a small joy,
After life was to pleasure, not there to annoy.

In the company of others he wallowed away,
Uplifted within, his mind fogging, going grey,
His last thoughts simmering,
His life disappearing.

He fell into a sleep of no return,
Not right away of this did others learn,
But once realised he was aside,
Sail cloth placed over him, peace to hide.

Seebaer Phillipse and Joannes Spandaun sat by the small fire,
Wishing to speak, wishing to pour out their desire,
As they talk between themselves they glanced at Ariaen again,
They had something of importance to say, did not wish to refrain.

"You have something to say," said Ariaen, kindly,
"I see it by the way you are looking at me so coldly."
Dirck and Wiebbe continued to examine the injured,
As others looked to the two young friends now inspired.

They were young seamen, on their first voyage for good wage,
Never before had they been to sea, waters so savage with rage,
"The fire should be bigger," answered Seebaer for the two,
"No passing ship is going to see this... thing: you have no clue."

HOLLANDIA NOVA, 1712

"Have you been this way before, in front of this coast,
Ever passed this strange land, its endless tracks of little boast?"
Ariaen said this as he rubbed his head wound beneath bandage,
A white band covering his forehead, he, withholding his rage.

"We are both new to the sea," answered Seebaer as he shifted,
Pivoting upon the spot, embarrassed by inexperience so gifted,
Said Ariaen: "I've been this way many times, many times have I,
I have seen the shore from far out to sea, before my very eye."

"At this point, just off the coast, a ship will turn to the north,
And then head towards its destination for what it is worth,
Only during certain months of the year will one travel so far east,
Far enough that they will have much on which the eye can feast."

"In all my times, traversing coast from here to the Sunda Strait,
I have seen many fires, always there, early night to late,
This land is inhabited by black men of which we know little,
But they must be tough to live here, not weak nor brittle."

"They wear nothing upon their bodies, carry spears and shields,
From knowledge they are very ready for war, plough no fields,
No towns or villages seen upon the coast, nowhere seen,
Of their religion we know not, but we assume them to be unclean."

"They surely skirmish with others from this land most regularly,
And they do this after reconnaissance most discreetly,
For we have not seen them anywhere near,
But they know of our presence and have no fear."

"A small fire will not do anything to encourage great assistance,
But to do nothing will not satisfy all here, I see by appearance,
So should I insist and a larger flame, evoke more smoke,
To openly want and invite that dreaded, black bloke?"

"So I shall do as I think is best and leave it at that for now,
When the dead are ready for burial, the fire we can grow,
Time will then be right to build it high, built it strong,
We shall cast a flame upon it, cremate the dead, I am not wrong."

"We cannot bury the dead, it is too much work, we have no tools,
When the time is right, the fire will be lit as though we are fools,
I hope the Kockenge will be near at that time to see signal sent,
I hope to draw them near, wish not our toils to be so easily spent."

Ariaen looked around the campfire to all those that had survived,
All except the drunks: and Harmen and Jan: wishing them alive,
"If no ship comes within the next five weeks then we rethink,
Think of something new, to rejoin civilization, regain that link."

A Solid coughing spell then concluded his views on the subject,
"What shall we do?" asked Seebaer, as though trying to object,
"A ship arriving at Batavia will learn of our situation,
They may link our fire with those missing, fill us with elation."

"I say five weeks of signalling, conserving as best we can our fuel,
Linking efforts to the time table I offered: we must all be mutual,
Ships will pass, but their precise day of passing: I cannot say,
I simply offer a guess derived from what I heard at Table Bay."

HOLLANDIA NOVA, 1712

"After the fifth week we will wait until the approach of summer,
Then make an attempt at launching our own boat, not to saunter,
I have no idea at this stage whether we shall be successful or fail,
But we shall require a good launching pad from which to set sail."

"I shall set out tomorrow," volunteered Seebaer. "I shall go south,
For one whole day and return," and to friend, opened his mouth,
"I'll take Joannes with me, we shall both go forth."
"Good," said Ariaen cheerfully. "Who will go north?"

Silence dominated the scene,
There were few who were keen,
"Seebaer and I," volunteered Joannes, "once we've returned,
Returned from the south, having found little or having learned."

"Even if finding something worthy you should still take a look,"
Advised Pieter as he then continued: "Water we need: a brook,
You might find something better in the north, learn from the south,
Be sure to take some cooked meat, to help sustain your youth."

"Something edible may also come your way,
But nearer the coast you must stay,
And ready access to the Ocean is needed,
And for God's sake, be careful, safety heeded."

Joannes nodded, "Very well. We shall go south, look yonder,
On return I shall venture north, to explore and to wonder,
For there will be much to consider and to formulate,
Of dangers and safe havens, much to extravagate."

Pieter added: "There are some blankets over there,
They will aid you by night when the sky, of cloud, is bare,
Courtesy of Willem and his collection, and so grows our store,
Take some with you, for weather dictates you need them more."

Joannes nodding acceptance with a smile,
His soul and mind ready to trudge mile and mile,
"Is there anything else that concerns anyone?" asked Ariaen of all,
"Not wishing to give voice of command, my desire is only to call."

"Yes, yes, that's it indeed, a call to organise our saving of soul,
We, seamen, even if young, deserted upon land to pay a toll,
And for what do we pay this price... possibly a test of our wits,
A test of conviction, to see whether or not we have merits."

"For the first time in our lives we must treat each as a brother,
So it shall be made clear: no one here is any better than another,
With different experiences and knowledge we must survive,
We need to collaborate more than ever, in order to stay alive."

The faces around the fireplace were easily read,
Each filled with agreement for what was said,
Willem stood up and sat down again beside his friend,
Ariaen, his father-figure, to aid where possible, to the very end.

"Shall I take meat to the drunks, the others?" Willem did ask,
"You're a good lad, Willem... in God's light to bask,
Considering others when they have done no work this day,
To aid those drunkards where they lay."

HOLLANDIA NOVA, 1712

"We shouldn't turn our back on them," said Willem. "Should we?
I overheard one of the other men saying he wished it was he,
Then the other wishing he too were drunk,
Wishing to be oblivious, their miseries sunk."

"Wishing to be drunk, and getting drunk, is not the same,
It is two completely, different things," said Ariaen, feeling shame,
For he should be as good as Willem, not so quick to blame,
But it was hard to do when so many were lame.

And then Ariaen added: "But you give me an idea."
He stood up. "We shall both deliver them meat, try and steer,
Steer them from their drunken ways,
And if not successful... maybe just rid them of their stays."

"And whilst we are amongst them, if they appear incapable,
We shall throw what they have of their stash from table,
Refuse them access so easily granted,
Upon ground or over the cliff it can be decanted."

"I'll come with you," said Hendrik, feeling wise,
"I hope we can easily, of their possession, prise,
Casting evil drink into the ocean will be my honour,
Be rid, too, of their foul, drunken stench, that evil odour."

Both forgetting it could be used to aid the sick,
Their heads filled with this desire and trick,
To end once and for all the drunken behaviour,
To be judge and jury, to be their saviour.

As expected the four drunk men were flat on their backs,
Sleeping heavily, a chink in their armour, their cracks,
Drowned of all reality until morning's first light,
They would be unable to do anything, and too few to fight.

It took quite a while to find the spare bottles of gin,
Bottles hidden, now found with a grin,
Willem too, enjoyed throwing the bottles as far as he could,
Into the night air, to smash or wallow and sink as they should.

The noise of breaking waves upon the platform below,
Were now a sweet pleasantness, on them to grow,
And on return to their fireplace they all drift off into sleep,
The gin forever gone, of its medicinal purpose they did not reap.

CANNIBALS AND SNAKES

6th June, 1712, the survivors rose with the dawning of the sun,
The fire almost out, being hard to start, but warmth finally won,
The day was a little cloudy, but quite cold despite this,
Their second morning in a strange land, the ship they did miss.

It was at this same time that Harmen and Jan woke to motion,
Greeted by a *thwack* in the bush not very far from their position,
Jan shook his friend and got up upon his knees,
Head lifted to see across the expanse of grass amidst light breeze.

A greasy plain for as far as the eye could see,
Dotted with shrubs, and here and there a tree,
And where the grass died away, nothing but a scorched turf,
A prairie of softly undulating ground, a bare and stubborn earth.

Dotted with eucalyptus to break up the monotony of the view,
There was not much else, compared to yesterday, nothing new,
"What is it?" asked Harmen as a rumble came from within,
"What do you see?" rubbing his eyes, a lack of smile, no grin.

"Nothing, I see... Harmen, quick," insisted Jan with emotion,
Rapidly upon his feet and running in the opposite direction,
Running as fast as he could, body carried by fleeting feet,
The fright within Harmen was so high that his heart missed a beat.

Such an action stole his breath away for a brief second or two,
He shot up and looked around, stunned, not knowing what to do,
Saw then, Jan, running away, a hundred feet or more,
He thought, 'what a coward', such action he did deplore.

And then he, himself, turned to see what was the matter,
A near-naked man with spear and shield, his mind did shatter,
An aboriginal looking, as though mystified by his appearance,
Seemingly astonished but unafraid of this white and large nuance.

Harmen was quick on his friend's heels, so quick, so fast,
Running for another hundred feet or more, this land so vast,
To then turn and see once again the dark flesh, this ill-clad man,
The aboriginal seeking contemplation: a spirit of his clan?

"Who do you think it is?" asked Harmen, largely pathetic,
"I don't know and I don't care," answered Jan, rather rhetoric,
Some scepticism taking strong hold upon him, he unsure,
"He's a savage; possibly a man-eater," to peace of mind no cure.

"Shall we try and communicate with him?" Harmen did say,
Jan looked at the man standing there, three hundred feet away,
The black contrast, doing little but glancing in their direction,
Both considering the others mind-set as well as their complexion.

"We should leave him be, of stable disposition we cannot rely,
And there's no telling how many others may be nearby,"
With that said Jan looked around, feeling much fear,
Making sure none other was trying to move to his rear.

HOLLANDIA NOVA, 1712

"I think he's alone," said Harmen, hopefully,
"Yes, probably," agreed Jan, within small depression, tiny gully,
Added Harmen: "He doesn't seem to be too concerned,
And he has a weapon—Hah! That's the first thing I learned."

"He's probably hunting food," concluded Jan who did recall,
"That creature we saw the other day, the one so tall,
Hopping across the ground in great stride,
The others won't believe any of this; they'll think we lied."

"Shall we return now? Pass on the news, get something to eat,
"Yes; let's go tell the others, and wrap ourselves in a warm sheet."
And so they commenced the short journey back to their campsite,
As a little cloud gave way, the surrounding area turning bright.

And as they moved along they shot glances back upon their tracks,
Making sure they weren't followed by any blacks,
No other way to describe them, as they would the whites,
No better way of indication than where reality bites.

Several gullies were crossed, those same passed the day before,
Several rock holes presented themselves, far from cliff or shore,
Sources of water to supply the survivors over the coming future,
Source of food now the torment, thoughts on which to nurture.

The sandplains now behind them as the pair continued their walk,
Painstakingly back to the others, to share information, to talk,
Their stomachs feeling less hunger than the previous night,
Hunger dissipating slightly with their short journey, their plight.

They then fell upon an old camp, easily drawing their attention,
Seemingly of good vantage, slightly higher in elevation,
The ground surrounding it easy to view, not by chance,
The Indian Ocean able to be seen via studying glance.

Being of higher elevation made it a good choice,
Good vigil all round available, many pros to voice,
There were also several bare spots where people had slept,
An old lean-to laid flat upon the ground, looking rather inept.

A single large tree provided shading,
And a large rock employed for making,
Making of tools, or grinding of food, weapons to improve,
A smooth concave surface in rock, a rock too heavy to move.

Said Jan: "It looks like our friend employed this place,
But it hasn't been used for a while: of it they did not efface."
"A summer camp," suggested Harmen. "A temporary hide,
I will guess acutely: somewhere for hunters to reside."

"Do you think they'll return?" asked Jan, looking over shoulder,
"I don't know; but we'll have to keep an eye open, be the bolder."
Harmen then bent down, lifting a large portion of stripped bark,
"Maybe they left some tools behind... look, see this mark..."

"What is it...?" Jan said as he turned to the silence,
He then froze too, in terror-stricken semblance,
Hiding coiled and peaceful beneath was a snake,
Which was quick to lift its head, its tongue to rake.

HOLLANDIA NOVA, 1712

Tasting the air,
A warning fair,
This his lair,
Be still, just stare.

Harmen had held himself well for the fright he had received,
Holding tight onto the bark in his left hand, hoping for reprieve,
He was in easy striking distance of the reptile and quite at a loss,
What should he do now, who in this situation was the boss.

The yellow scales of the six foot snake gave it a menacing look,
Not to mention the position it held: Harmen's legs shook,
Ready to lash out with a bite to Harmen's leg or arm,
Harmen's head rang in alarm, but he needed to remain calm.

Jan could see that Harmen wasn't going to move anytime soon,
He considered the situation, rather light headed, ready to swoon,
"I'm going to pick up a fallen branch, Harmen, to distract... it,
Don't move; for God's sake... keep still: it could leap, bite or spit."

Jan moved around towards the rear of the snake,
He took up a long branch, tested it with a single shake,
The snake turned its head to look upon Jan, just out of reach,
Harmen then moved his foot, a prayer he did preach.

Ah, a mistake, moving it a little further out of the way,
In an instant the snake turned to have its say,
And it struck out at the movement, as fast as can be,
Sinking fangs into the flesh of the calf, its venom now free.

Retracting his fangs it departed the scene, leaving the dread,
Jan's empty effort to beat down upon it hit the hard earth instead,
Harmen bent over in more shock than pain,
Grabbing hold of the wound with the palm of his hand in vain.

He then removed his hand and probed with shaking finger,
Over the site of the wound, some venom seen, digits linger,
"Damn; damn that thing!" cursed Harmen as he fell upon his arse,
"Of all the blasted luck, this worthless land: no benefit, no class."

"And now bitten by... what? Hiding in ambush, being sly."
"I never saw such a thing," a shocked Jan said in reply,
Jan gazed out, looking towards where the snake had slivered,
And then upon the frightful look of his friend, poison delivered.

"What am I to do?" shrieked Harmen, a cry, a shout,
"The poison... we have to suck it clean out."
"Quickly," prompted Harmen. "Get a knife."
"I don't have one, Harmen… how am I too save your life?"

"At the camp; get Dirck or Wiebbe," Harmen did yelp,
"Quickly, Jan, or I'll be dead. Run for your life, get help."
"Shouldn't you come with me? I can manage a carry."
"No; but you're right... I can walk. Quickly; let's not tarry."

Harmen got to his feet and started to move as fast as he could,
Close behind his friend Jan, not really knowing if he should,
Moving with speed, to be saved before the poison did react,
Before his body gave out: the poison they needed to extract.

HOLLANDIA NOVA, 1712

They weaved in and out of the scrub, no given graces,
Pushing through the tea-tree, growing thick in places,
There was more than a mile to go over rough terrain,
In the general direction of the others, aid to gain.

The sweat commenced to pour from them both as they did move,
Jan, more than Harmen, believing he had more to prove,
To save his friend: something he had to do, this he knew,
And the distance behind them grew and grew.

Harmen suddenly halted and drew his hands to his heart,
He fell suddenly like a sack of potatoes, there to depart,
Straight to the ground in an instant, death overriding all will,
A grotesque contortion painted upon his face, he lay very still.

A MATTER OF COHABITATION

Seebaer and Joannes had commenced their exploration,
Going south on morning's first light, filled with inspiration,
Taking nothing more with them other than some small portion,
Burnt meat from the night before and full of good intention.

They had decided to try and return by last light,
In this way they could share in a campfire at night,
Again replenishing their energy before another long day,
Heading north for further exploration of coastline that lay.

The two had only travelled less than half a mile,
When they came across what afforded them a small smile,
It appeared to be a small beach fronted by gentle sloping ground,
Which extended out onto a rocky sea floor and lucky to be found.

They took note of the area for the importance that it offered,
Not so much for the ability to launch a boat, [if they bothered],
But for the landing of a boat from rescue ship, if one came near,
To see their signal fire, close enough to the coast, able to steer.

They spent little time here, wishing to be on their way,
More concerned in covering ground, not in causing delay,
And by midday their feet were rather tender,
Excessive reason to saunter, not to meander.

HOLLANDIA NOVA, 1712

The effect of wet feet shoved either loose or tight,
Into the shoes of a previous owner, were not quite right,
Beggars can not be chooses in time of need or desire,
Offering little comfort but protection in times so dire.

The way south, as too, was presumed for the north,
Was full of many species of wildlife, many brought forth,
Mostly of feather: whistle, squawk; fluttering upon the breeze,
Of ground: ants, centipedes, lizards, beetles, and pests to tease.

"Our food won't last long, Seebaer," said Joannes out of the blue,
Trying to provoke conversation as they continued, speaking true,
"No. But time will be our reward, not all times will be bad."
"Maybe not, but there's plenty of time to be had."

"If no ship passes our way soon," Joannes did say,
"Ever more time than we can bear will come our way."
Said Seebaer as a few more steps were taken: "I was thinking...
These insects and beetles may be edible; and no, I am not joking."

Joannes screwed up his face as he considered the idea,
Of crunching into a beetle; of poison, of choking; the fear,
Pressing one between his teeth until its innards came rushing out ,
Faeces disturbed from its arse, onto his tongue and round-about.

"I mean to say," continued Seebaer, "the savages upon this land,
Well, they've learnt to survive, taken the surroundings into hand."
Joannes considered this for a moment, contemplating, being fair,
"Seebaer, you know what, you might have something there."

"Yes indeed; struck a chord you have," Joannes congratulated,
Nodding his head in an act approval, though not entirely elated,
Seebaer: "No better way to learn than from savages: so obvious."
Joannes stopped dead in his tracks "What? You can't be serious?"

"Why not?" said Seebaer as his shoulders shrugged up and down,
"They've lived here long before any ship saw this land so brown,
They survive day to day, and haven't yet attacked,
They have so much knowledge, so much experience well stacked."

Said Joannes: "But we haven't come into any contact as yet,"
Not knowing of Jan and Harmen, their encounter so met,
"What if they're hostile?
What if they live a life so vile?"

Seebaer: "If they're hostile then we are already dead,
The only way is to befriend them, to use our head,
Search them out, share in their secrets in order to survive,
Do all that we can to stay alive."

"Look, the sun is directly above us," Joannes said of time of day,
"We should return with the news we have; what do you say?"
Replied Seebaer: "I honestly believe it's our only way,"
He continued: "To seek out the savages, find out where they lay."

"And if a ship doesn't find us within the next few months or so,
Then we will have to trust the savages, in this I know,
Like the VOC trusts in those of Batavia and beyond,
But of eating beetles, insects and other, I'm not truly fond."

HARD CHOICES, SOFT MEN

It was just after midday, time for something to eat,
Time for the survivors upon the cliff to gather and meet,
Gathering at the place transformed into a temporary camp,
A small fire burning dull, unable to ward off cold nor cramp.

Kindling was quickly added and the flames stirred into motion,
A pot of water filled from a nearby source, to concoct a potion,
To boil what may be considered tea by some,
But others confess it's tasteless, bland and glum.

What meat remained was wrapped well, stored back in a barrel,
Sealed with a cover, placed in the shade, so not to spoil,
Gerrit Jongbloet, one of the drunks from nearer the cliff ,
Walked up to them, stood there, dishevelled, cold and stiff.

"I've come to see if I can get something for the others to eat,"
Said Gerrit, a shameful look of despair upon his face to meet,
All of the others looked upon him and then to one another,
Before shifting their view to Ariaen, as though their mother.

"You'll have to wait, Gerrit," said Ariaen. "The sick come first."
Hayman, the man with broken legs, voice cracking from thirst,
Quickly voiced his opinion, "Give them nothing, I say,
Give them nothing at all; for forgiveness they should pray."

"What is it to you, old man?" scolded Gerrit,
"You'll be dead soon," such tone carrying no merit,
Cursed Hayman: "Damn you to hell!
I wish, from the cliff, you all fell."

"Enough!" and Ariaen was upon his feet so fast. "You shall eat,
But be warned; you and your friends have choirs to meet,
You must make amends, help with the work, all day through,
And there will be no more drinks for any of you."

Said Gerrit. "Our supply is finished, only a few bottles we had,
For a rainy day... now gone. So ashamed I am, but also glad,
We all feel rotten to the core,
What can I say: what more."

"Every day would be raining in your eyes," scoffed Hayman,
Said Gerrit: "Okay, I was wrong, but I smell meat in your pan,
We are hungry, too, all of us are willing to conditions meet,
We are part of the crew, we deserve to get something to eat."

"Be warned, Gerrit, there are no other bottles left for you,
Every bottle was thrown into the sea, and nothing you can do,
You must all help or receive nothing. Be a man, not a whelp,
And, Gerrit; we are more than you, it would be wise to help."

"Is that a threat, Ariaen?" said Gerrit with a frown,
Responded Ariaen: "Make of it what you will, don't be a clown,
Discipline must remain if we are to be successful in our plight,
Stop squabbling amongst ourselves, ahead is a fiercer fight."

"Very well," said Gerrit, "I shall tell the others, but please,
Give me some food, go back with a full hand to appease,
The others are still drunk but will be ready to start work soon,
Will these terms be acceptable; to commence early afternoon?"

"It is, Gerrit. We're also going to rest, for the work is hard,
The salvage operation is almost complete, to every inch and yard,
A signal fire will be our next concern, the dead will be cremated,
This will prevent the spread of disease, and dull the work created."

"I understand," said Gerrit. "I'll go and tell the others and return,
To get some rations, give time for the others, of mistakes to learn."
Gerrit departed, leaving the main group to continue with cooking,
To allow them their rest, to avoid their stares, so sour looking.

A noise then came from beyond,
A familiar voice, of which some were fond,
"It's Jan," said Dirck. "I'd know his voice anywhere."
They all listened carefully and it came again upon the air.

Muffled by the background noise of the sea,
And some thick scrub of tea-tree,
Dirck yelled: "Jan, over here."
"Help me. I need help," came the voice of fear.

"Did he say 'help'?" asked Dirck: for he heard but could not see,
"Yes," replied Pieter as he, too, stood. "Quickly, follow me."
Dirck and Pieter raced off through the scrub as fast as they dared,
Calling out, closing the gap, their positions shared.

When finally upon him they saw Harmen upon shoulder,
Draped over Jan him like a rag doll, much there to ponder,
Though there was no time to be slow and easy,
For set in stone was that sense of urgency, the need to be busy.

There was Harmen, most of the colour drained from his face,
Jan let the body fall, and he fell to his knees, falling from grace,
Said Jan between deeply drawn breaths, tired right through,
"He was a good friend, but there was nothing I could do."

"What happened?" asked Dirck, seeing the man dead,
"A snake bite," said Jan, and with the word came much dread,
Unveiled now many looks of despair,
Poor Harmen had fallen upon a snake's lair.

Little thought had been given to such a danger,
Void of all contemplation, but then, none were eager,
But now more than ever they needed to tread warily,
To be always on the lookout, to walk most carefully.

"Come, Jan,' comforted Dirck, "you aren't to blame for anything,
There's so little that you could have done, absolutely nothing."
"If only I had a knife," said Jan, "I could have cut his wound,
Sucked the poison from within him, the bite was so easily found."

"It's finished now," said Dirck. "Come. We'll carry Harmen now,
Take him to the fireplace. Have a rest. Then you can tell us how."
"No," protested Jan. "I'll carry my friend, I feel the need."
"We'll all help," said Pieter, "together as one, we're all agreed."

GOD'S DAMNATION

"Help, come quickly," came the voice,
"What now?" said Wiebbe, wishing he had a choice,
"No, Wiebbe," said Willem, pointing towards the cliff, the west,
"Over there; it's Gerrit," Willem remained calm, doing his best.

"Quickly, help," gasped Gerrit as he raced towards the fireplace,
"What's wrong, Gerrit?" asked Wiebbe, for the worst he did brace,
He was feeling as though an injustice had been served,
Harshly dealt by Gerrit and the other three, not what he deserved.

"Cornelius Brouwer has fallen, off the cliff and down the slope,
I think he hit his head. He isn't moving. I need help, need rope."
Wiebbe looked down to the three men in his care,
"I can't leave these men, I don't dare."

"Look…. take someone with you… someone capable,
Not your friends; and see if he's hurt, if his condition is stable."
"I'll help," said Willem, standing and preparing himself for duty,
"You stay there, Willem, and cook the food, be my deputy."

"We all need nourishment. Hendrik, you and Gerrit go,
And see what can be done, I'm confident you will know."
"Aye," obeyed Hendrik in as quick as a flash,
Grabbing Gerrit by the arm, to be off at a dash.

The three men were taken to the accident site, to the very spot,
Willem sat back down and stirred the meat and peas in the pot,
Wiebbe looked down upon the open-eyed threesome in his care,
But in all true admission, was he being fair.

"This is a fine mess, Willem. Two calls for help, three wounded...
That's me and you, boy; that's it... just the two of us, surrounded."
Wiebbe to Willem: "I don't mind telling you that this very minute,
Right now is the loneliest I have felt in my entire life; I do admit."

Pieter, Dirck and Jan could be heard moving through the scrub,
The harsh land always there to remind, to lash out and rub,
And no sooner at the fireplace, and Wiebbe was at their side,
Ready to assist where he could, ready to give aid, ready to abide.

They laid the body of Harmen upon the ground, unshrouded,
And in full site of all there, and the three wounded,
Who in their state could only contemplate their near future,
It being the same, no medicine or sacred potion to nurture.

Of the three that lay upon the ground with bandages and splint,
Only one was unfamiliar with Harmen, no friendship to mint,
But he had come to know him during that first morning,
After the Zuytdorp had wrecked, during its unfavourable mooring.

The body of Harmen was laid upon the ground,
Wiebbe knelt down beside him, there being no sound,
Dirck was opposite and looking rather solemn,
Knew that he was gone, and without requiem.

HOLLANDIA NOVA, 1712

And then the silence was broken,
Some words were softly spoken,
Said Wiebbe: "It's times like this I wish I were a priest,
To give comfort, a comforter of the sick, to be worthy at least."

Wiebbe looked Dirck in the eyes and understood his frustration,
For neither was a doctor, each held another station,
But both had intelligence, smarts you could not burn with wick,
Enough to understand the rudiments of providing aid to the sick.

It comes naturally after many years at sea where men fall victim,
Victim to scurvy and diseases of the tropics so heinous and grim,
Where the shells of men fall victim of God's own vengeance,
Or so it would seem by all outward appearance.

The silence was then pushed aside as Jan commenced stirring,
Standing there with something to say, unsure how; a warning,
He gave the news which all were dreading to hear,
"I saw a savage, a naked man with a shield and a spear."

The others tending the injured,
Those lying upon the ground hence hindered,
Even the breeze, all stopped to listen to the greatest dread,
To learn what was new, of what was to be said.

"I saw one of them, and Harmen too,
He was dark and stood erect, as though with nothing to do,
Holding his ground and eyeing us with hunger in his eyes,
I could see and hear his mind in play, I tell you no lies."

"I could see his wish to boil my flesh for eating,
My soul to roast upon a fire, my flesh basting,
His thin shell showing him hungry, and on flesh he relies,
His eyebrows provide shelter to those deep, dark eyes."

"The eyes, the evil that they cast in our direction,
Their look of greed, on community no reflection,
If it wasn't for the fact that he was alone,
He would have been after us, with spear or stone."

"Was he all of that, Jan?" asked Pieter, still standing beside him,
"He was indeed, and much more," concluded Jan, no fat to trim,
"Then we must prepare for the worst," said Ariaen at last,
"Several knives have been salvaged, their quantity not vast."

Said Dirck: "They'll do little against the thrust of a spear,
And what other weapons does he have near?"
"They're savages," reminded Wiebbe. "What can they possess?"
"They've survived here," advised Pieter. "But let's not guess."

"They've lived upon this land, naked to the world, and survived,
Survived the elements, beast; the snakes; yet they're still alive."
"And the damnation of God," said Marinus from upon blanket,
Rubbing his good hand across his broken ribs, much pain met.

"They're God's creatures too," said Willem, voicing his opinion,
Said Jan: "Savages like them don't have religion,
I saw the evil in his eye, almost close enough to smell his breath,
I wouldn't wish to confront a group of them for fear of death."

HOLLANDIA NOVA, 1712

Gerrit and Hendrik then returned with bad news,
Cornelius had died in the fall from the cliff of views,
Having hit his head upon a boulder,
As well as dislocating his shoulder.

Said Hendrik: "We dragged his body to where the others lay."
He looked upon the form of Harmen, not knowing what to say,
"Poor Harmen," feeling saddened,
Seeing no blood, now confused: "What happened?"

Said Jan: "He was bitten by a snake and died,
But right until the end it was life that he vied."
And as this was spoken all eyes fell to the ground,
Fear now embedded in all, firmly and sound.

DEATH

Before dusk had arrived upon them this day,
The survivors had gathered at the site where the injured did lay,
Seebaer and Joannes had returned to the smiles of friend,
Happy to be back, but of their journey no end.

It was a miracle in itself, this feeling within,
The safety they felt being amongst this group so thin,
All of whom were in the same predicament shared the same fears,
Suffered the same miseries, shed the same tears.

It wasn't as if they'd be absent for any great length of time,
Or returning into the arms of a loved one so prime,
It was the comradeship that they needed, the comfort of another,
Another fellow that shared their will to live, happiness to smother.

Both men listened intently to the story told,
Of how Cornelius had fallen to his death, body now cold,
How Harmen had come to grief,
Of their efforts to aid the injured and give relief.

Of the savage seen beyond the scrub where the land was bare,
Like a motionless sea, undulating plains, savage and unfair,
Land bare of life other than trees which sucked the land dry,
Of the sheer lack of moisture and how by summer they would fry.

HOLLANDIA NOVA, 1712

But the survivors provided each other with stability,
A small and yet rigid, unyielding commodity,
This, the centrepiece of their communion,
Their togetherness, their union.

Only two drunks, Jacob Albertsz and Jacobus Nuyts, out cold,
Possibly a gin bottle hidden too well: they were crafty and bold,
Remnants of broken bottles laying around,
Beware the sharpness of broken glass to be found.

Surprising it was that they were still alive,
But their poor condition didn't allow for them to thrive,
Despite this they had been provided warm blankets,
For pity and handouts they were like magnets.

Blankets to keep them warm, cold rolling in from the sea,
Where cloudless nights sucked warmth from man, beast and tree,
How on earth did the savages survive such weather,
Walking around naked as they did in skimpy leather.

Cornelis Lieffers then appeared from his work,
His devotion to keeping busy, none to shirk,
Bringing another bucket with him filled with fresh water,
Water scooped by hand, by gallon and quarter.

"Cornelis, young friend," said Ariaen to the young man, not old,
"You work too hard and need to rest; consider yourself told."
"I fear the thoughts within me will surface and explode,"
Said Cornelis, not wishing his mind to erode.

Willingly letting his guard down, his emotions to betray,
His exhaustion taking hold, the foundation now lay,
"You need to rest, nevertheless," continued Ariaen. "Behave,
There have been too many deaths already, you I wish to save."

Ariaen looked at the man coming of age: "Will you sit and join us?
Seebaer and Joannes have returned with news; on them let's fuss."
"Is it good news?" asked Cornelis, giving approving, his vote,
"We've found somewhere that may accept a sturdy rescue boat."

"Can this be true?" asked Cornelis, "But not to sail a raft."
"We don't think so, Cornelis," said Seebaer, no good as such craft,
And with a downturned eye: "But we intend to go to the north,
To search for another place, one of great worth."

"And work you've achieved alone will provide us with wood,
Enough wood for a small boat; I'm sure of it; it will be good."
"Yes," said Cornelis, his heart lifted. "Enough to make two,
And drag it from platform to embankment is all we need to do."

"Yes, indeed," said Ariaen. "There is much to do tomorrow,
So go with Seebaer and Joannes, of you they wish to borrow."
"They'd be faster with two," said Cornelis. "Wouldn't they?
And what of the work here? I think I should stay."

"We are plenty," added Ariaen. "And in number we grow,
Gerrit, Jacob and Jacobus will be joining us tomorrow,
To be put to work... isn't that right, Gerrit, good fellow?
With us combined the work will flow."

"Yes," said Gerrit, looking at Cornelis, into his eyes,
"The other two will have sore heads, but work... this we prise,
But with a little food and water they will do just fine,
And as for myself; my labour is yours, not mine."

Cornelis smiled and nodded, "Okay, I'll go; adventure to meet."
"Great," said Ariaen. "Now sit down and have something to eat,
Rest those weary bones of yours, for tomorrow you journey far,
And when you all return, your stories will make you each a star."

"It's just a day trip, isn't it?" asked Cornelis, now unsure,
"You didn't hear?" prompted Pieter, now leveraging his lure,
"Hear?" repeated Cornelis, unsure of where this was leading,
"Of Jan and the savage?" said Gerrit, who continued his feeding.

"No," said Cornelis. "What savage?" and the story did not derail,
He was told of what had happened, to the very last detail,
Said Pieter of this plight: "So you see,
In order for victory we need at least three."

Cornelis nodded acceptance, not wishing to let the men down,
And Willem consider, a desire to follow this example now sown,
To be willing and strong enough to do all that it does take,
To survive and devote oneself, to harden conviction, to bake.

Said Joannes: "I think, too, we stop thinking of them as savages,
We are not amidst a war here that rages,
For if a ship fails to come our way,
We may be forced to remain here, to forever stay."

"Our only means of survival,
Would be of an allies arrival,
Of this sunburnt land they are native,
And for us this may prove to be relative."

"Only time will tell, Joannes," said Ariaen. "Only time,
But you're right, one day this land may rub off on us like rime,
We to be encased in all it has to offer,
With the land itself to become its brother."

"But for now we need to explore towards the north the most,
Where much coastline is known to exist, of this, our host,
Many ships have used this coast to mark their progress,
Three hundred miles of it, if correct, to softly caress."

"And I'll go too," said Jan, looking at the others. "I can't stay here,
Not with my friend having departed from this world so dear."
Said Ariaen: "We'll be saying our goodbyes soon enough,
I'll understand if you don't wish to stay, for it must be rough."

"I have said my farewell, carrying him upon my back,
For many hours in the heat of the day, courage he did not lack,
I wish that winter was here already," and he kicked at the dirt,
His shoes well-worn, trousers dirty and shabby, a torn shirt.

"It's upon us," said Ariaen, scratching at the bandage he wore,
That covered the gash in his head, itchy and sore,
And looking out over the ocean he said "It has just begun,
And of all the wishes you make, only a single you have won."

HOLLANDIA NOVA, 1712

Jan: "If it wasn't for the heat, that snake might not even exist,
If colder than now it may be away in a hole, not out to persist,
I guess there is much we don't know about this land,
Everything needs to be learnt, and knowledge is grand."

"The ways of one snake isn't necessarily the same as another,
Take that creature, the one I saw jumping, over and over,
In great bounds across the ground... that in itself is unbelievable,
How can such a thing exist? And there it is, achievable."

"We believe you," confirmed Ariaen. "If you wish to go north,
Well, we'll not stop you, but encourage you, for what it is worth."
And to change the subject he looked to Willem. "How's the meat;
Your peas; your broth? My stomach is waiting for it to greet."

"Ready," said Willem, proud as could be,
Looking around at smiles, pleased to see,
Happiness so remote with death all round,
So hard to avoid, so easily found.

Some may draw on this situation as condemning and sad,
A shortened existence on earth, terrible ends, this was bad,
But others would grow and see the many opportunities to take,
Shake the defeat from within, pour courage, confidence to make.

Moulding a new life for themselves,
Upon this new land as though picked from shelves,
For now they would consider the idea as suggested,
Joannes and Seebaer's thinking in mind, it to be digested.

The bounds of survival were commencing to surface,
For those with the courage to take it, to enforce, not deface,
Grasp ideology into an open palm,
To remain clear-thinking, to remain calm.

Of the man that had fallen from the cliff, a man clearly rotten,
He had fallen to his death and now practically forgotten,
He'd been so simply dragged over to the pile of dead,
A pile that currently existed on the shoreline platform of dread.

The mass of flesh was beyond them all to fathom,
Life wasted, death to young and old, taken from earth's bosom,
No clemency, no difference between command and structure,
Whether seaman, woman, or child: nothing now to nurture.

Of the little children, only one was found and placed at the pile,
The others had been lost by way of the sea, the sea to defile,
The waves taking the fragile forms of human remains,
To a burial site which none could claim, and the unknown stains.

What one does not know, must be learnt,
And here, now, all learnt must be clearly burnt,
Burnt to memory, new tricks and sites grasped,
Refuse to allow their lives hit hard and rasped.

That evening there was much to reflect upon and reflect they did,
But mostly in silence, behind a screen of security well hid,
They were all too tired to do much about anything at all,
So they lay, asleep, half asleep, to gather their wits, not to fall.

HOLLANDIA NOVA, 1712

Silently contemplating the future, but also needing much rest,
Regards of little slumber or a lot, they must do their best,
Gather their energy, be ready for the morrow,
To greet the day, to be enlightened, or be hit by sorrow.

GANGRENE

7th June: The drunken men were now completely sober,
No alcohol within their system, not part of any fibre,
They could see the error of their ways, or maybe not,
But suffering a little from the shakes, there on the spot.

Here the new dawning of a day,
With the sunlight a fresh wind, but not all day to stay,
Dragging along a mass of cloud, mostly clear, a few quite dark,
But currently no sign of rain nor lightning and its vicious bark.

With broken bottles left upon the ground to stain,
A visual memorial there to remain,
To that single one who fell to his death,
Upon platform so far beneath.

These men sat there beneath the rays of the sun,
Unmoving, unstirred, but under mantle of social gun,
To appease the desire and need of the others,
Not yet truly accepted as brothers.

One other thing did greet them with the rising of the day,
Another body was relinquished to God from the fray,
Francisco Roelofsz, with the broken leg and punctured gut,
His ghostly spirit, his soul, from his body now cut.

HOLLANDIA NOVA, 1712

Hayman Jorisz pulled his fingers from his bandage,
Placed them beneath his nose, the smell, of mind, to ravage,
Then withdrawing them quickly for the smell was overpowering,
The most horrid thing he'd ever smelt, his fingers quite disgusting.

The wounds smelt of decayed meat, of death, pure and simple,
He was gangrenous, terror coursing through him, to ripple,
Seebaer, Joannes, Cornelis and Jan had gone to the north,
But the others were there, to hear his news brought forth.

With an upturned nose he was about to request aid,
To wash his fingers, though not the emotion of being afraid,
When he saw approach both Jacob and Jacobus, men of disgrace,
Hayman simply watched in silence, hatred written upon his face.

He knew deep down that his legs would have to be amputated,
Cut off from above the knee, from thigh separated,
What was there to relieve the pain, for the pain to stop,
There was no gin... it was gone, every last drop.

Wasted upon drunkards who were weak, not strong,
Whom could not handle the disaster, knew not right from wrong,
He would show them, that he could hold back the cries of pain,
Prove his true convictions, to put on a strong face and be vain.

And the two men walked past him, glancing down but briefly,
Willem, Pieter, Ariaen, they could see,
Hendrik, Dirck, Wiebbe and Gerrit, there too, upon one knee,
And they continued their approach as each did agree.

"Sit down," said Ariaen in invitation. "Have something to eat,
Take the weight off of your feet,
There isn't much but we are hoping to secure food later on today,
Some shellfish and maybe other supplies to come our way."

Jacob was handed a piece of bark, a plate on which sat food,
"Thank you," said Jacob as he sat, for nourishment, in the mood,
Pulling the slightly curved piece of bark into his chest,
To guzzle it down and give his grumbling stomach a rest.

"And for you, too, Jacobus, a small meal."
"Thank you," said he, for hunger he did feel,
Gerrit looked upon his so-called friends who had corrupted him,
Forced him to accept the gin, to feel as though he was the victim.

"How do you both feel?" Gerrit did ask, as they ate their food,
Jacob: "I'm fine." Jacobus: "Me too." As they did sit and brood,
"And why wouldn't you be, you scum!" cursed Hayman, thinking,
Thoughts on the pain to be endured, of his legs and the stinking.

"You take all the gin and scoff it down, and now you come here,
You've not done a single days work, and behind backs you sneer,
And now you partake of our sustenance as though nothing at all,
You each have a tremendous amount of gall."

"It's from all of us," said Ariaen, indicating the food they shared,
Understood the hate, not the inability to forgive, why anger flared,
"Let's hear no more of it, we are in this together, one and all."
"It's easy for you to say," said Hayman, his back against a wall.

HOLLANDIA NOVA, 1712

Tears slowly filled his eyes before drying in the breeze,
As it blew in from beyond one of the seven seas,
"I'm to be amputated and there is no gin left; no wine; no beer,
No medicine or anything else other than sheer fear."

Gerrit stirred and spoke softly to the man in anguish,
"I have a bottle, saved for you; you can have it if you wish."
The two drunks shot a glance apiece at Gerrit, full of hate,
"Where is it," stabbed Jacob, extremely obsessed and irate.

"Enough! YOU SWINE!" a curse that fluidly ran,
"Sit still, Hayman," ordered Wiebbe as he raced over to the man,
Hayman tried in vain to claw his way to Jacob, to kill with hate,
"You have sinned," said Gerrit, wishing to seal the bastard's fate.

"And so have you," answered Jacobus, under the collar quite hot,
"Gerrit is one of us," spoke Ariaen. "You two men, as yet, are not,
You've been given food and water, now earn the right to speak,
You prove only one thing; your greed for gin: you're weak.

Jacob held out his hand for all to see, shaking out of control,
Unable to stop the tremors from within, it was taking its toll,
"I'm not a doctor," said Ariaen. "Only you can overcome desire,
You helped yourself to the gin, so you must help yourself aspire."

"I can't," said Jacob in all sincerity and regret,
A look of terror upon his face, one never to forget,
Juice from peas and meat dribbled from the corners of his mouth,
"I must have it; please. I have no spirit left, it's all gone south."

Said Wiebbe: "There are others in need of it more than you,"
He leant forward and smelt the wound: what he said was true,
Sorrow filled his face as he stroked with great compassion,
The forehead of Hayman, to he would go the gin, the ration.

"Pieter; Dirck... will you help me?"
"What is it, Wiebbe?" asked Dirck, standing to see,
"It's time," answered Wiebbe with face, undefined and solemn,
"It's time to take these legs off; that is the problem."

The sorrow within Hayman's eyes was the look of an innocent,
A child, a hideous crime about to be committed most indecent,
The look upon Jacobs was similar, but filled with deceit,
Capable of doing anything he could for gin and its receipt.

Silence... the men moved to the task in silence,
Forgetting their food and water; now filled with patience,
Thinking only of the poor man about to be operated upon,
Wishing and hoping that he could and would remain strong.

They moved Hayman, away from the others, half mile or third,
Towards the south where the screams would not be heard,
Ariaen went too, with embers for fire carried by Willem: his task,
For it was his job, handed to him, this, of him, they did ask.

A fire which was to be employed in preparing the cutting tool,
To prepare the knife, a job suited to any man, child or fool,
It was large enough to be handled as a cutting device,
Could be used on bone and flesh; to chop and slice.

HOLLANDIA NOVA, 1712

Willem returned to get some cloth and some rope,
And a little extra kindling for the fire amidst fading hope,
Several small logs would not go astray,
And these he grabbed whilst he pray.

And as he returned he passed Gerrit who was off to retrieve,
To retrieve the hidden bottle of gin, for Hayman to receive,
Close enough to see, but far enough so not to be heard,
Followed Jacob on his own errand, an outright coward.

Willem focussed upon his task, ignored what he saw,
To ready the fire and bandages for that man so poor,
Gerrit stepped out amidst broken bottles, of location to take stock,
To find that hidden, last bottle, the gin beneath large rock.

He got down upon his knees and commenced to excavate,
When a noise caught his ear, but he turned too late,
He saw Jacob standing over him face screwed up tight,
As he brought a large rock down upon Gerrit from height.

The strike killed him instantly, Gerrit's fate sealed,
Jacob grabbing for the bottle which had been revealed,
The neck now sticking out, a sore thumb: one not to shun,
The best site Jacob had seen his entire life, second to none.

He wasted no time at all and soon had it open, ready to drain,
Swallowing in great gulps all that it held, unable to refrain,
Before long it was empty, he just could not stop,
As though a flagon of water, drained of every last drop.

Jacob suddenly turned and saw Jacobus standing there,
Having followed soon after, unwilling to simply sit and stare,
Seeing that Jacob was up to no good, not out on walk for fun,
"You bastard," scolded Jacobus. "What have you done?"

Jacob looked down at Gerrit's body, the empty bottle released,
But Jacobus was referring to the gin, not the deceased,
Jacobus: "It's gone, every damn drop. You drank it all, its gone,"
All spoken before the reality of the situation hit him hard as bone.

"You've killed Gerrit, that's a sin,
Killed him for little more than a bottle of gin."
"I had to... I..." stammered Jacob, on feet so unsteady,
For the drunken state to befall him he was very ready.

Back at the fireplace, Willem had returned to secure more,
Hendrik looked to the boy, confirmation to score,
From far out, in the distance: "Willem, did you hear that sound?"
Willem: "God! It's Jacob, and Jacobus; Gerrit! The gin, found!"

Hendrik looked down upon the sleeping form of Marinus, asleep,
Oblivious to what was going on, no longer able to weep,
Having been awake and in pain for most of the night,
He had finally falling to slumber, to Hendrik's delight.

"I'm going to see what's going on; stay here, near this bed."
"Here," urged Willem, thinking straight from the top of his head,
"Take this," and handed the knife to him before racing off too,
Towards Wiebbe and the others, where impatience grew.

HOLLANDIA NOVA, 1712

Hendrik took the knife without second thought,
Raced towards the commotion, conflict now sought,
Falling upon the scene in what seemed to be a moment's notice,
To see Jacob and Jacobus fighting, neither the novice.

Each was rolling around upon the ground, Gerrit unmoving,
Gerrit steady there, of his condition there was no need to sing,
Blood running freely from the wound upon the top of his head,
Like a script, all about him, it was all so easily read.

"What have you done?" said Hendrik in disbelief as they struggle,
The fight: Jacobus near the ledge, Jacob trying to strangle,
Jacobus now clawing at the earth, he suddenly slipped and fell,
Hendrik was utterly astounded, this was sheer hell.

Jacob turned, his eyes glazed over by the gin, his mouth in a snarl,
Civilization gone from his face, the truth he could not gnarl,
He was no longer a man but the devil possessed,
From all manner of human sanctity he had regressed.

With the bloodied rock still in hand he circled Hendrik now,
Motioning him to fight, of surrender never to bow,
"I have a knife, Jacob," advised Hendrik. "You have no chance,
Put the rock down, forget this fight, this death dance."

"We're here to help, all of us; I am... here. Let me help you."
"I curse you... damned, bloody fool. It is all through,
Besides, I have more than you," and Jacob held up his hand,
"I have the rock, right here; my iron, soon to be your brand."

He looked into Hendrik's eyes and raced forward,
The rock in motion, he footing most awkward,
And the stumbled as Hendrik stepped aside,
Jacob falling to his death, no wind to ride.

Hendrik just stood there, disbelief within,
His mind unable to calculate all of the sin,
This was not how man was supposed to survive,
This was no way for man to live, to live and thrive.

What manner of evil could possess another to commit such an act,
Such a heinous crime against his fellow man, the point of fact,
It then suddenly dawned upon him that he too had plenty to repent,
For his vicious treatment of others before now was easily spent.

He had tried to become leader, to have the ability to sway,
Sway judgement over those under his command, to have a say,
But now... he didn't want it; that is the way it should be,
He was glad that Ariaen had received more votes than he.

He was glad to have lost to a better man, for Ariaen was strong,
Day in and day out he had proven not to be wrong,
He was a good man with a clear vision for the future,
This leader was one, not to oppose, but one to nurture.

It's what was needed, a strong man to lead a volatile group,
A bunch of men whom had much to recoup,
Ariaen was helping them all find their way in this new world,
So cast upon a land with misgivings that swirled and whirled.

HOLLANDIA NOVA, 1712

Hendrik could only whimper to himself, of the needless slaughter,
Feelings of sorrow filling him like a carafe is filled with water,
He would have to come to grips with it all, that had come to pass,
All that undone at the seams, this lesson learnt from this class.

AMPUTATION

Hendrik returned to where Pieter, Dirck and Wiebbe were readied,
For the amputation, removal of leg, for it to be burnt or buried,
Willem was tending the fire and checked over the supplies,
So placed neatly beside Wiebbe, and on these, much relies.

Ariaen sat silently at Hayman's head,
Ready to assist where possible at this makeshift bed,
Ready to obey orders as they were given,
Of true conviction, to be hard driven.

"Willem," said Wiebbe, "Thank you, but it's time for you to go,
Back to the main fire, there is no more for you to know."
"But I can help—," began his protest,
"You've done enough," concurred Pieter. "Time for you to rest."

He smiled at the boy. "Go and get yourself something more to eat,
Or better still, prepare something for all of us, solace to greet,
For we'll be hungry after the job is done,
Even if unable to eat, a little is better than none."

Willem nodded acceptance of the task and turned to depart,
Bumping into Hendrik as he stepped away, to make a start,
Forgetting Hendrik's intervention upon the two drunk men,
The others asked Hendrik for information, there and then.

HOLLANDIA NOVA, 1712

"They're dead," said Hendrik in a half daze,
Not quite believing the words as the others did gaze,
Gaze upon him with open mouths so large,
The words tripping their ears, scrambling, as though to barge.

"Dead?" repeated Dirck, unsure of what he heard,
"All three," nodded Hendrik. "I know it sounds absurd."
Pieter stood, "Maybe you're wrong, maybe we should look."
A hand lashed out: Hayman, grabbing Pieter's leg, and shook.

"The bastards deserved to die," said Hayman, being blunt,
"No one deserves to die in this place," said Pieter, to affront,
Pieter looked down upon the man to be operated on soon,
"No matter their faults," came his lecturing tune.

"They're dead," repeated Dirck. "I saw two fall to their death,
And Gerrit has a wound to his head, a deathblow, easily read."
"Where's his body?" said Pieter as he grilled,
"Trust me, why don't you.... at the cliff where he was killed."

Pieter got up to attend, to see for himself, to do his best,
"Pieter," said Dirck. "Don't go, let him lay in peace, at rest."
Dirck looked at Hendrik, "There's nothing that can be done.
Our task now is to help Hayman; for a victory to be won."

"You're right," said Pieter as he took up his position,
To prepare for the task of holding the man during the operation,
And they were the last words for a while,
As Hayman's legs were unbandage: there remained no denial.

The smell of the gangrenous leg hit them all hard,
The mass of swelling revealed, putting them off guard,
The discolouration taking full effect upon their hidden emotions,
The fractured bone having broken the skin, its many lesions.

Wiebbe was to do the cutting; Dirck and Pieter were to hold,
Hold tight Hayman's arms and upper body, no need to be told,
To restrict, for him to be as motionless as possible,
For what was about to happen was extremely horrible.

Dirck stayed beside Wiebbe so that he could take over the task,
Of hacking through the bone if the need arose, he only need ask,
Hendrik sat at the ready at Hayman's feet,
Feet soon to be separated, no ceremony to meet.

"No, Hendrik," said Dirck, cautioning the man to the requirement,
"Get beside Pieter and help with restricting, for ease of treatment,
Hold firm the the upper leg... the thigh; keep it still,
We must act swiftly: an hourglass in seconds to fill."

Wiebbe had already separated the task from his friend,
Mental application, to deny any affiliation, sanity to defend,
He would separate the two so that no semblance did exist,
To shut out all that Hayman may say, to do all he could to assist.

He applied this thinking to actual practise,
To deny the reality of his being less than a novice,
In his mind the body to his front was unfamiliar,
As peculiar as a small tree trunk, a column, a pillar.

But his mind found it hard to dissociate flesh from friend,
About to deliver much pain of which no one can defend,
Pain and suffering beyond all contemplation,
And no way of creating a substantial distraction.

But he had conviction of mind,
Though not easy to find,
And no amount of screaming would stop him from hacking,
No amount of struggling would prevent him from slashing.

Once started the operation could not be stopped,
To be done in the shortest time, as he saw and chopped,
And before the screaming was netted to ear,
Leather was placed between his teeth on which to grind and tear.

Willem was sitting beside the fire, cooking as he sat,
Thinking of what was to unfold: alone, with no one to chat,
His only wish was for Hayman to survive the surgery,
To pull through this serious operation and its savagery.

But his thinking was obscured by a cloud,
Once the screaming started so loud,
The thick leather between Hayman's jaws having served little,
Of purpose it failed; was insufficient; its effect broken and brittle.

Willem could only wish for silence to reign,
For solitude to appear once again,
It was shear torture, the sounds of pain and torment,
The screams arrived in an unbroken cycle, in sight, no relent.

Tears then welled up within Willem's eyes,
The noise too much to bear, and here he cries,
He rolled over on his side, into a tiny ball,
Clutching palms tightly upon his ears, the noise to stall.

And yet the screams came reverberating,
Like the devil to unguarded soul, penetrating,
There was nothing that could compare,
With those fifteen long minutes of despair.

The screams finally coming to an end,
Silence to his ear beginning to blend,
The reverberation to a standstill,
No longer that awful shrill.

Willem was thankful that it was over, no more lament,
Praising the Lord that he had stopped the torment,
Thanking God for answering his prays, of his reply,
For bringing him silence, and he wiped his eyes dry.

It was only minutes later that Pieter appeared,
At the fire, his forlorn face, of peace, so sheared,
He stepped next to the hearth,
A look of solemnity, one of death, not birth.

"What is it?" asked Willem, thinking he knew the answer,
But afraid to say it out loud, his inbuilt censor,
"Hayman is dead," answered Pieter. "The pain was too much,
Even for a man of our nationality, a man most assuredly Dutch."

HOLLANDIA NOVA, 1712

And Willem began to cry once more for it was his fault,
He, praying for an end to the screaming, and here the result,
It was his prayers to God without poise,
For an end to the torturous noise.

Yes indeed, it was he, Willem, that had asked for Hayman's death,
For it to be delivered this day, Hayman drawing his last breath,
"What? What was that?" came a tired voice as Marinus awoke,
Waking from slumber, having missed all, and he spoke.

Still half asleep: "Who's dead?" he did prattle,
The wind commenced to pick up a little,
Blowing harder than it had twenty minutes before,
Pieter's answer muffled by the wind as it tore.

WILLEM

Seebaer, Joannes, Cornelis and Jan were making good progress,
As they continued towards the north voluntarily, not under duress,
When their apprehensions were finally alerted,
Of the tension, no longer diverted.

The basic lay of the land was similar as it was to the south,
As it was to the west: experienced, not by word of mouth,
Although in the west there was slightly more for the eye to see,
But still a barren wasteland, a semi-desert, they did agree.

It was most inhospitable, commencing from the limestone cliff,
And in towards undulating, featureless sandplains, an ongoing riff,
A virtual monotony, thickets of acacia and banksia easily found,
Mostly sparse with some thickets, strewn across the ground.

Alike to islands upon a vast and open sea,
But often little happiness, no ounce of glee,
Perches for the birds and shade for some critters,
Those small like ants, and larger still, those with stingers.

But there was a tranquillity,
Though absent of any familiarity,
A margin between cliffs and barren landscape of trivia,
Of chalky earth covered in salt-tolerant heath and acacia.

HOLLANDIA NOVA, 1712

The limestone platform continued along the coast,
As it was near the shipwreck of the Zuytdorp, for the most,
There appeared to be no permanent water source in the area,
From what the men could see, as scarce as trees on a glacier.

But the aboriginals knew the whereabouts of rock holes and soaks,
Well endowed with knowledge, relatively nomadic these blokes,
Water, liquid gold, needed for life, for life on which to binge,
Such water hides were five miles away, not on the coastal fringe.

The approaching storm had been building for the past three hours,
Weather, the instrument of torture and bliss, it held many powers,
"We'll have to make shelter, soon," said Joannes to all,
"We may be hit by a sudden and fierce squall."

"I agree,' said Cornelis, shifting his blanket upon his shoulder,
It being tied with thin rope [a loop], he now feeling colder,
"Where to, that's the question," stated Seebaer most realistic,
"This cloth we have isn't much against this wind, far too rustic."

Seebaer: "We need to find shelter; be smart, not dumb,
Asked Jan: "How far do you think we've come?"
"Why?" Cornelis did joke: "Do you want to turn back already,
Afraid of a little wet and hard work, on your feet unsteady."

Jan took the comment the wrong way, of tongue and mishaps,
Interpreting it as an insult, "What? scared; me, lazy perhaps?"
He felt injured, assaulted in some way,
But the feelings were not there to stay.

"No," winced Cornelis. "I was simply commenting... look,
It doesn't matter. I too would prefer to accept a clear brook,
A nice shelter, a log cabin, an oil lamp,
But even these we lack back at camp."

"You're right," accepted Jan, "I'm, sorry; please."
Cornelis was hence more careful to tease,
"Well, we need somewhere," said Seebaer, "maybe a large tree,
"And the sooner, the better, if you ask me."

Cornelis: "We've come about ten miles is my guess,
But then again it could be more, or a lot less,
It's so hard to tell when there isn't any sun,
Until these clouds have up and run."

Seebaer: "My feet are as sore as hell,"
"Mine too," added Jan, wishing to tell,
"Courtesy of the shipwreck and these damn conditions,"
conclude Cornelis. "So kindly spent upon us, with no restrictions."

"Let's try heading inland," he looked to Seebaer, for agreement,
"There will be trees there, will there not?" this a statement,
"One of worth?" questioned Seebaer with little emotion,
Hunched over and shielding his face in open palm action.

And the heavens opened up and the downpour commenced,
A storm which would rage for many hours, of great expense,
The suddenness of the downpour precipitated by a lightning strike,
That shook the earth they were standing upon, not one to like.

HOLLANDIA NOVA, 1712

"Come, let's go; quickly," voiced Cornelis as he lead the way,
Stepping off into the unknown without further delay,
The rain fell in buckets, the gullies filling up temporarily,
Water flowing away from undulating ground, and not sparingly.

Across sandplains and into the sea, soaked to the bone,
Torrents of water falling over the cliff of limestone,
And miles away, back at the camp, the same did adhere,
A great misery which worsened, though nothing left of any cheer.

Willem was hunched over and seemed very pale, a grave matter,
The shelter they had struck providing sufficient shelter,
Good protection from the pouring rain,
But of the penetrating cold, little warmth to gain.

The boy was shaking like a leaf and looked like hell,
Sweat started to fall from him freely, a ringing of bell,
The men gathered together, refusing to be beat,
Endeavouring with all their ability to harness body heat.

Only Dirck and Marinus remained apart, but not to suffer,
Quite a few feet away, half asleep and laying beside each other,
A large rock pile at their head where red hot embers from the fire,
So placed in order to maintain, keep them from a fate most dire.

With no embers to play their part,
Fire would be costly to restart,
Willem's symptoms had come out of nowhere,
Older boy, or young man, it seemed so unfair.

Wiebbe held his palm against the boy's head and shook his own,
"He has a fever; from what I don't know," and Willem did groan,
Hendrik: "This damn land and the savages upon it,"
Seemingly concerned for his own future, upon the land he spit.

Hendrik pulled away, possibly not wishing to catch the fever,
The sail above his head leaking slightly, to slowly deliver,
Several drops of rain penetrating the fabric and falling,
Falling upon his head, folding fingers into armpits for warming.

"No," said Ariaen. "I don't believe that. No one has a fever."
"So he's the first," said Hendrik, "That's all; the first to suffer."
Willem was clutching at his stomach, a small telltale signal,
He was in much pain and seemingly a little delusional.

His eyes darted, looking here and there,
Not at anything in particular, not to stare and stare,
It was then that he vomited all he'd eaten that day,
The meat, the peas, nothing in his stomach would stay.

"Poisoned by his own hand," said Hendrik. "It's greed,
That's the answer; poisoned, on too much he does feed,
God knows when one is being greedy, selfish beyond call,
It stands to reason that to the devil he shall fall."

"It's nothing to do with poison," said Pieter, ahold the boy's arm,
In an effort to offer some comfort, as though to protect from harm,
"The food, you fool," said Hendrik sarcastically,
He's always alone, feeding himself, so full of folly."

"I know not, Hendrik," spat Pieter out of character,
"The boy has had no more than any here, he's no gluttonous eater,
It's not greed; we have all had the same,
He's playing by the rules, playing the game."

"Did anyone notice anything strange?" asked Wiebbe of others,
All shook their heads. "Dirck; Marinus; look here brothers!
Did you notice anything wrong with the boy?
There must be good reason; calculated thinking we must employ."

"What?" came Dirck's reply, seeing with sudden surety,
That Willem was in difficulty,
He yawned a little, stretched his arms wide, on his side he lay,
"What's that? What's wrong with Willem, what did you say?"

"You tell me," answered Wiebbe. "Did you see anything wrong,
With the boy earlier on? Anything at all that does not belong."
"Not, not a thing," said Dirck. "What symptoms does he display?"
"He's vomiting, has a fever, and in much pain; not at all okay."

"Maybe it's something he ate," came the reply from Dirck,
Upon Hendrik fell a look; a haunting smirk,
He then looked Pieter and Ariaen in the eye,
"I told you, didn't I?"

Wiebbe tried to gain Willem's attention,
Lifting his head and checked his vision,
Staring directly into him, seeing nothing at all,
Nil response, and he did softly call.

Wiebbe: "Willem; do you hear me?"
"Of course he hears, and he can see—."
"Shut up, Hendrik," the death stare sealing Hendrik's mouth,
Hendrick's conviction soon to be drained south.

"There's nothing," said Pieter. "Let's put him down,
Make him comfortable, until something further is known."
Said Wiebbe: "There may not be a later,
Whatever he's suffering is rather sinister."

Later that night, when the stars came out to greet life on earth,
Clouds now past and rain from the storm drained through turf,
Drained via gully and swallowed up by the dry land,
Invisible creatures could be heard, each song a brand.

Songs which were free for all to listen,
Sweet pleasantness of sounds, so bright they glisten,
Stretching as though the night and over the folds in the ground,
Mating calls amongst them made, and mates found.

Dirck and Marinus were asleep on the far side of the hearth,
Ariaen and Pieter fast asleep, near Willem, for what is was worth,
Wiebbe, on the other hand, was wide awake and listening,
To the sounds all around him, a loan ear to christening.

Here he tried to decipher what he could of the beetles and grubs,
Insects and nocturnal animals, many species amongst the shrubs,
He'd never realized such music existed,
It truly could not be resisted.

HOLLANDIA NOVA, 1712

It seemed to him that the boy, Willem, had recovered sufficiently,
For he to be left unattended, to be checked intermittently,
A little colour had returned to left and right cheek,
His pulse was normal, fever gone, no sweat of which to speak.

He was sleeping comfortably and with his arms across his body,
No longer was he crunched up in a ball nor looking shoddy,
No longer holding for dear life to his stomach real tight,
Whatever was wrong was now put to right.

Wiebbe wasn't an educated man, but neither was he stupid,
He'd learnt a little of medicine, but of love no cupid,
Could tell the time of night by looking to the heavens above,
And of men and their sarcasm he did not truly love.

It was in this way that he could see that the morning,
Would be upon them soon with a magnificent dawning,
The storm having passed them by in their shelter,
And no real issue did they encounter.

He stood up and stepped from the shelter,
Headed towards the higher ground, solace to enter,
Through some thick scrub and following his intuition,
Some scratching noises then heard, their cause now an ambition.

He'd gone several hundred feet when he came across the ground,
The proposed camp site suggested by Jan earlier on, now found,
For the ocean could be seen quite clearly, as advised, from there,
But he did not loiter, he continued on his way from that so bare.

And then within minutes he came upon another great site,
Good for a camp, more rewarding than the other, just right,
Many thoughts then swept his mind, of life and death, disease,
Of cures, medicine, food and water, of his feelings it did tease.

The scratching noise now forgotten, he continued to wander,
Walking around, back to camp, under arm a little tinder,
He set the wood aside and bedded down once more for sleep,
But could not, his mind full of theory, no solution to reap.

The early morning had brought Ariaen and Pieter to the fire,
Wiebbe poking it with a stick, for a breakfast he was dire,
A breakfast of peas and shellfish,
The blandish and plain, dull dish.

Pieter asked Wiebbe: "Have you been up long?"
"Not long," answered Wiebbe. "I was feeling a little… wrong,
I couldn't sleep and so went for a walk for awhile,
I was deep in thought, but not more than a mile."

"I thought I'd get the fire restarted after the raining,
We don't have much dry wood remaining."
"It'll be enough," remarked Adriane, "enough for several days,
At least until the sun can loan us some wood-drying rays."

"I was thinking," said Wiebbe, "to make another camp,
Further away from where we are, a bit of a revamp."
"What in God's name, for?" queried Ariaen. "Why not stay."
"I went to where Jan and Harmen ventured the other day."

"I came across a great spot which offered a little protection,
Protection from the wet, and a rise in elevation,
From there we'd have a good view of the ocean,
Better to watch for, and see, a passing ship in motion."

"And just beyond that is another position,
A place for any sick, like a hospital, a good location,
Said Ariaen: "You're concerned over Willem, aren't you?
But you shouldn't be. He's not plagued; there's nothing to do."

Wiebbe: "Not just him. Look at Marinus. He seems well enough,
But what if he turns gangrenous... on some it will be rough,
They shouldn't all have to suffer that heinous smell,
Some of them would prefer to confront the fires of hell."

"Look," began Pieter, "I have no objection,
It may even alleviate a little tension,
But if we're going to have more than one campsite,
Then I think I should be with the sick, to help make things right."

"I see no issue," said Wiebbe. "Dirck and I will take turns,
Help look after any sick and there fever as it burns,
Regardless, it's a duty which must be performed,
But there is one other thing on which I'm concerned."

"And that is?" asked Ariaen, of information to fetch,
"A lookout near where the sandplains begin, for miles to stretch,
Just one thousand feet from the sandplains there's a place,
An old camp: Jan told me of it... told us all directly to face."

Said Pieter: "Ah; where Harmen was bitten by that snake,"
"Yes, that's right. We can maintain a vigil, a vigil to take,
Upon the natives we watch, see what they do, how they act,
    Consider it an early warning, time for us to react."

"It already has a large tree nearby for preparing food,
    For the hanging of carcass, providing good mood,
And there's a large rock there, seemingly used for grinding corn,
    Of the natives it was purposely born."

    "There must be food nearby,
    Something on which we can rely,
    Of food a descent supply,
    For our survival this does apply."

"We must explore all options and keep our eyes open,
    Staying in one spot will summon bad omen,
We need to commence with the laying of traps,
And strands of fibre are required, for the making of straps."

Ariaen: "Wiebbe; there aren't enough of us for three,
    Two camps possibly, just open your eyes and see,
    Having any more will not, our situation, mend,
    Do this and we will all be condemned."

Wiebbe protested aloud: "That's rather a strong word,"
Ariaen: "Nevertheless, you suggest placing the sick in a third,
Either yourself or Dirck, in a camp with Marinus: the sick,
    You're burning our candle, with more than one wick."

HOLLANDIA NOVA, 1712

"These numbers: that accounts for three, with me, together;
And then with Pieter; that leaves seven, no other,
Is this entirely necessary?
Will it be but temporary?"

"We would only need two men at a time at this place,
The site near the sandplains; where animals jump and race,
The others could maintain the camp nearest the sea,
Watching for a passing ship; give us hope, fill us with glee."

Pieter agreed with this: "I think he's right,
It's against my better judgement, but this I shall not fight,
To separate Willem from the remainder is awful,
But I see the logic in it, for I am no fool."

Ariaen was silent for a few seconds and then nodded acceptance,
"Very well. We'll tell the others, despite possible askance,
As soon as they wake, we'll tell them simply,
Get things on the move and commence immediately."

"There is one other thing," said Wiebbe. "We must burn the dead,
Burn them now, where they lay, in preparation, to heaven be lead,
I don't see the point in dropping them over the cliff top,
It's a waste of energy… besides, where does our humanity stop?"

They each nodded in silent agreement, feeling that it was right,
They could not afford an epidemic, a rampant disease to fight,
Their lives were important and so they would act fast, be brisk,
The dead would forgive their grievances, understanding such risk.

SHORT HUNT

Seebaer and his companions fared reasonably well,
In the conditions that had fallen upon them: bequest from hell,
Considering that all they had was a little sailing material,
And several blankets to summon warmth, to health an arterial.

The tinderbox they had carried with them was of no use at all,
No dry material for which to start a fire, one could only mull,
And fire at such time when they needed it most, sanity to repair,
Such measly food; their stomachs feeling heavy despair.

The storm had played havoc with them, so rough its wake,
Strong and fierce, the earth did seem to shake,
They were thankful that it hadn't lasted as long as they dread,
Of good spirits there were so few to be read.

The misery of the men wasn't so much contagious,
for all were suffering the same, though not quite outrageous,
For misery of large weight won't allow a man to continue,
On a journey of little reward, A body of retainers, this retinue.

In most places the cliff proved to be impassable,
Therefore the gathering of shellfish, they were not able,
And as no other means of support availed itself,
Left to dream on, with visions of fruit-bearing land to tilth.

HOLLANDIA NOVA, 1712

There was no rockhole nearby, nothing passed,
The supplies they did have, had not last,
An empty water-carrying device they had, yes they did,
Constituting an old pot with a loose piece of cloth as a lid.

But in this they were fortunate, for its neck was wide,
For lack of water they no longer needed to [archaic] bide,
Huddled around the old pot, fully replenished as new,
For due to the night's rain its level... it grew.

With blankets draped around them, they considered their options,
"We have to return immediately," stated Seebaer, head in motion,
There being no argument against such a vote,
Only more nods of the head, of clear understanding all did note.

"We all agree to that," said Jan. "Against my better judgement,
But what choice do we have amidst this aggrievement."
None could see an ounce of argument with that,
As they huddled in blankets, there they sat.

Seebaer nodded, "I'll lead the way if you wish and will start..."
The sudden fall of silence attracted all eyes to dart,
Ears erect, intent on hearing sound that Seebaer did not mention,
To hear what it was that had drawn Seebaer's attention.

"What is it?" asked Joannes as he whispered,
Seebaer held his finger to his mouth, all voice had disappeared,
And then the noise came again, not so far away,
Something moving towards them, seemingly to stray.

Possibly something close to the ground,
Dragging something along, something it had found,
It was a rustling noise of slow approach, coming straight,
The crunching of debris beneath a heavy weight.

Seebaer stood up, half crouched, now straining to look,
In the direction, his stance, and to the core he was shook,
Most temporarily his eyes grew large,
Not knowing what to do, either sit or simply charge.

The others looked upon him in terror, afraid for what it might be,
A savage, or a group of them, something heinous he did see,
Who knew what this land help in secret ready to be unleashed,
Against them so unvarnished, so unceremoniously dished.

"Seebaer, what is it?" Joannes asked again,
Feeling the need and desire for news, even one of pain,
"A large creature with small legs; as big as Willem that's no lie."
Said Seebaer, placing his finger against his lip, for silence to try.

Seebaer: "Listen to me carefully and trust in what I say,
Do you trust me this day?"
Everyone nodded, yes,
What was to happen was anyone's guess.

"When I say go you must all stand and take up a stick or rock,
Kick with your foot if you must... its head to knock,
Throw a blanket upon it, do all that you can,
All of us together, to the very last man."

HOLLANDIA NOVA, 1712

"He will be slow because his legs are so small,
It is quite short, not very tall,
Are you, each one ready...
NOW!" and not a soul was unsteady.

The four men rushed to their feet,
To confront a new creature, one to meet,
Before them a wombat, so large and plump: of which none knew,
A great mass of flesh ready to be made into stew.

Blankets were thrust upon the creature so brown,
Stones and rocks taken from the ground and thrown,
A large rock lifted by Cornelis delivered a shocking blow,
Upon the creature's neck as it moved, blood to flow.

It moved hurriedly away as other blankets were recast,
Picked up again, and the chase was on, action fast,
The commotion of the hunt was in full swing,
All in complete disbelief at the sight of this thing.

It was something that looked like... nothing they'd seen before,
This could be a great victory, a resource, one not to ignore,
Colourful language filled the air as orders flew,
And within all their anxieties grew.

The energy now exerted was depleting,
There thoughts mainly focussed on eating,
An adrenalin rush for fresh meat,
Overwhelming and not discreet.

The wombat was under great stress,
The attack a shambles, a great mess,
Blankets thrown upon him not budging,
With rocks and sticks, taking a beating.

The men closed in on the creature and lashed out,
Raised voices in the commotion giving a shout,
Several beats to the head connecting well,
And it was then that Seebaer fell.

He fell upon it with the only knife,
To him bonded, as though a wife,
It penetrated the animal, taking its life,
Gone now was the wombat's strife.

But Seebaer wished to make sure,
Stabbing again, and again, more blood to pour,
And they knew that the creature was dead,
In its motionless state this was easily read.

The creature was now skewered from mouth to anus,
An action necessary, but most grievous,
A pole procured from sturdy branch,
The animal still bleeding, but no wish to stanch.

The pole was carried between two of the group,
On their minds, collectively, that of chunky soup,
But with no fire, unable to bring water to the boil,
There was nothing to do but commence their toil.

HOLLANDIA NOVA, 1712

And so they commenced their journey,
With wombat on stick, not a gurney,
The men changing position from time to time,
Taking more rest breaks as their exhaustion levels did climb.

It was very tempting to bring their return to a momentary halt,
For small portions of the beast to be eaten raw with no salt,
But there would be no luscious flavour from fat of meat,
Nothing from chin to wipe, no great satisfaction to greet.

The trek back was of the most tiring,
The men were exhausted, hard was their inspiring,
And without proper nourishment they tired all the more,
Not an ounce left, all feeling quite sore.

But they had caught food for the first time, a great gift,
And this alone did aid their spirits, to uplift,
Pondering the meal to come, they almost felt like singing,
Pushing the thought from head, of their feet and the stinging.

And as the morning grew into early afternoon,
Seebaer looked up, saw something to his front, and not too soon,
Something that gained his immediate attention, for he saw smoke,
Thoughts all good, of optimism it did provoke.

"Do you see that?" shouted Seebaer for the others to look,
His finger pointing in the direction, a feast to cook,
For the camp was not far away,
Spirits lifted from minds growing grey.

"A signal fire!" presumed Jan, breaking out into a run,
In order to see for himself the white sails of a ship, saviour won,
Coming to the cliff's edge - but there was none,
Now at tethers end, feeling completely done.

"Don't; Jan," yelled Seebaer. "No ship is expected so soon,
Not until at least the eleventh of June,
Today's the eighth,
Calm down and just keep your faith."

"Leave him, Seebaer," said Joannes. "Let him alone,
He'll find out soon enough, his feelings to dethrone."
"But maybe it is a ship," said Cornelis with a smile,
"No, Seebaer is right," said Joannes, not in denial.

Cornelis: "Then what is it?" peering round, a look of lead,
Said Seebaer: "It must be the dead."
Bodies burning away,
Being rid of the stench and decay.

Back at the camp, Pieter moved up to the cliff ,
The wind askew, of stench they could not whiff,
With an outstretched hand he offered Ariaen a gift,
In his hand he held a pipe, emotions to lift.

Said Pieter: "For the tobacco you carry in that small box,
You might like to clean it first. I found it wedged between rocks."
"Thank you, Pieter," Ariaen smiled as he turned the pipe over,
Of tobacco he was a great lover.

HOLLANDIA NOVA, 1712

He turned it in his hand,
Studying it closely, it make, its brand,
Seeing whether or not it would hold up to being smoked,
"It looks sound. I'll clean it tonight," and he was stoked.

"You should consider yourself lucky, through and through,
That only a few other men amongst us smoke as you."
"I guess so," agreed Ariaen. "But share I must,"
And turned to glance upon the flames, their past was sheer dust.

As the flames licked up the cliff's face, its surface to rub,
Hendrik stepped up from beyond some scrub,
And nonchalantly said, "It might concern some that the fire,
Will attract the attention of the savages, a situation most dire."

"My God," answered Ariaen with a little panic, "You're right."
Hendrik: "But, alas, if we are to signal a ship, a fire we must light,
So I guess it's of little concern,
Of any repercussions we shall soon learn."

And he walked away, continuing on back to the campsite,
"That's the first, real thing I've heard him say that's truly right,"
Said Pieter, to Ariaen, "and he just walked away,
Before I could tell him; before congratulations I could lay."

Ariaen shrugged: "Savage this, native that; no matter,
I guess we will encounter each other sooner or later,
It won't make a great deal of difference... do you think?
Aren't we already beginning to sink?"

"No, not really," answered Pieter; wondering,
He looked over to where Wiebbe and Willem were standing,
"They don't seem to care too much,
I believe they have much love within, to give at a touch."

Ariaen: "Maybe they haven't given it much thought,
Or maybe they only share, one to the other, feelings sought,
After all, Willem currently has needs; Wiebbe does too,
Their lives will be expensive: they are far from through."

Ariaen looked into Pieter's eyes,
Looking deeply, to uncover secrets, as though spies,
"Maybe we should be looking to the natives of this land,
They've lived here for their entire lives, with it, hand in hand."

PORPHYRIA VARIEGATE

"It's a sorrowful sight... very depressing," said Pieter as he looked,
Upon the flames leaping into the air, the corpses as they cooked,
"You're right," answered Hendrik and turned away, heading back,
Back to the small camp, to find food on which to snack.

He wasn't gone long before screaming out a mass of obscenity,
In respect to what confronted him, a breach of security,
For just beyond the fire, where the meat was stored,
Came a vision which seared and scored.

Their supply should have been tightly bound with a cover,
Maintained in the shade, at all times, shade to smother,
He found it was bare to the air around,
And not in the cool shade of hole dug in the ground.

The others came running, within them a feeling of fear,
Willem following up, at a slower pace, from the rear,
Willem feeling weak and mentally drained,
Of all his usual outpouring energy, nothing remained.

"What is it; what's the matter?" asked Ariaen drawing alongside,
Now next to Hendrik, waiting for a response, for his to confide,
Marinus looked over from where he lay, drowsed from slumber,
Finding it hard to see what was the matter.

"The meat," pointed Hendrik. "It's spoilt; every last chunk,
Every strip, and bone. Damn it to hell, now we're sunk."
A mass of flies of the likes they had not seen before,
Had swarmed upon the meat, more and more.

The cover to the prize had been dislodged,
By the wind earlier on, malignancy not dodged,
There were ants in the thousands, line upon line,
Coming and going, a banquet ready, a meal so fine.

"Maybe we can wash it," said Marinus, wishing to give aid,
Hoping to contribute something to the group as there he laid,
Feeling lazy, drawing his rations in water and food,
But performing no task or responsibility, but in the mood.

"Wash it!" cringed Hendrik. "Are you mad?
It's contaminated, beyond salvage." so much worse than sad,
And someone had left it out of ground,
Not immediately picked up, whereby it should astound.

"I'm afraid he's right," said Wiebbe so surely,
"Of course I'm right," came Hendrik familiar tone so severely,
Wiebbe: "We can't take a chance on it, there's no more to eat,
Willem has been bad and it could well be because of this meat."

"Willem is young and fragile, unable to take the abuses of disease,
Not like a fully grown man, to his body, of immunity, to lease."
"Ah!" yelled Hendrik. "The boy, it's his fault; it is, it is,
The meat was stored by his action; the fault is his."

Willem then stepped upon the scene, the uncovered meat,
The others surrounding the fire, upon their feet,
The dislodged cover bearing all to the world,
Accusations to be dodged before hurled.

"It wasn't me," said Willem, a pleading look within his eye.
"I placed the cover upon it; I did, that's no lie."
"It's okay, Willem," consoled Pieter, "It's not your fault;
It was the storm; don't feel distraught."

Hendrik fell upon his haunches, it was taking its toll,
"Blast, it. The boy should have placed it into the Hole,
The boy should have checked it, thrice each morning,
And thrice each night; to double check it, of its proper storing."

"It's too late now," said Wiebbe. "What's done is done."
"Yes," agreed Dirck as he moved over to Marinus, laying prone,
"Throw it into the ocean and forget it, its final day has been spent,
The last thing we need is to be divided by discontent."

Their faces were rather solemn,
This was no small problem,
Hendrik stared at Willem, accursedly, now and again,
A snarl, an upturned lip, of this action he would not refrain.

His face was betraying his feelings,
No one else around to make clear rulings,
The large fire behind them still burning,
The flames simmering, long from smouldering.

And then the miracle,
Amidst the debacle,
Seebaer was the first to be heard,
By the noise, not a spoken word.

"Seebaer," said Wiebbe, standing on his feet,
Going up and slapping him on the shoulder, happy again to meet,
So happy to see all returned safely, smiles upon their faces,
All in good spirits, not lacking in good graces.

"By, damn," said Ariaen. "What manner of creature is that?"
"I wish I knew," answered Seebaer. "But not an overgrown rat,
We caught it this morning, and have been carrying it ever since,
I'm sure you'll be willing to eat it, no need for me to convince."

Jan then said: "We also saw the smoke from the fire,
But no sails upon the ocean on which to admire,
And we don't see you dancing a jig upon the edge of the coast,
So quite sure there's no rescue on which to boast."

"You're right," said Ariaen. "We burnt the dead; all in one place."
Jan: "With or without sermon; with no steadfast grace?"
"Without. Who here is a priest or other man of the cloth?
No one, that's who; no single person able to [archaic] doth."

"So be it. I've already said my goodbye, before Harmen was cast,
Cast into the flame, to be drawn into heaven, forever to last."
"Go and say another," said Ariaen, understanding the torment,
Of friendship torn apart, in life comradeship so cast in cement.

Jan looked around and stepped away, his errand to do,
Not another word passing his lips as he disappeared from view,
"So; what news do you have?" asked Pieter, changing the subject,
Bringing joy back into their world, of sadness to deflect.

"No real news," said Seebaer. "We found it hard to continue,
The conditions were too trying, into the fire we flew,
We decided to return and have brought back this... thing,
Meat for us all to eat as you can see, to eat like a king."

"We'll have to hang it," said Wiebbe. "Skin it for the fur."
Ariaen: "Not here, Seebaer; we've been rather busy and eager,
And decided on changes, to make survival better... more relative,
And to increase our chances of communication with the native."

"Waste of time," said Hendrik, "if you ask me."
"It's necessary," said Adriane, standing up for Wiebbe, to agree,
"We're going to maintain three campsites: three."
"Three," voiced Cornelis apprehensively.

Cornelis pondered: "We can't even manage to care for one,
How are we going to manage three; how's it to be done?"
"We have to try," said Wiebbe. "There's a good position,
A little further inland... not far, one allowing for good vision."

"We can see the ocean from there, it's well suited,
Any passing ship will be easily spotted,
A little past that and we'll have another,
For the sick. For this plan we are relatively eager."

"The sick?" prodded Seebaer for confirmation,
Wiebbe: "Willem was gravely ill last night, with no solution,
We don't know the cause, no way of knowing what was wrong,
It may have been the meat. He still feels weak, not fully strong."

Seebaer and the others looked to Willem who seemed well,
As though, lifted from his shoulders, was a cast spell,
Seebaer looked him up and down,
A smack of the lips and a frown.

Wiebbe: "He had a fever and stomach pain, was extremely weak,
Seemed to forget himself for a while; worsened as we did speak,
He's a lot better now, as you can see, a great reliever,
So we know he doesn't have a disease or tropical fever."

Seebaer looked at Willem, "You look pale, too," he added.
"Even paler last night," said Wiebbe, "for nought he was avid."
Seebaer took a pace forward, "Do you know what I think?
With those symptoms, for him to feel so low, to sink."

Wiebbe was utterly flabbergasted, hit in the head with rock,
He was beside himself and in a little shock,
That Seebaer should know the cause of Willem's discomfort,
And in a matter of seconds, and with such little effort.

"He has Porphyria Variegate," concluded Seebaer. "It's not good,
I've seen it before, strikes mostly after childhood."
He looked to Wiebbe and back to Willem, not abstractly,
"Exactly as you say: suited to these symptoms exactly."

"The more severe cases can suffer hallucinations; skin damage,
Diarrhoea, muscle weakness and seizures, all hard to manage,
Blistering of the skin and scarring, and sensitivity to sunlight,
It will not be good come summer, when the sky is so bright."

"Fever and sweating is also quite commonly found,
Possibly unsteady upon his feet, not secure and sound,
Willem; your family... does anyone suffer like this, do you know?"
Willem answered, a good reply to this gauntlet of words to throw.

"Yes," said Willem. "My mother suffers badly of hallucination,
And much pain, weakness and fever, her ruination,
She's a drunk and cares little for me: but that name,
The doctors said what you just said... the very same."

Seebaer repeated the words of before: "Porphyria Variegate,"
"Yes, that's right," confirmed Willem, of confusion, no hate,
"Well, I think that's your answer," said Seebaer, a little pleased,
"And what's the cure?" asked Wiebbe, for answer to be released.

"There isn't one," said Seebaer, "but relief can be given,"
Sounding of little confidence, to home none driven,
"How is that?" prodded Pieter, so that, for the boy, he could care,
Wishing to aid Willem, for his life to be fair.

"Plenty of food," and those words prompted much traction,
Ariaen: "We do as suggested by Wiebbe, let's get to action,
Wiebbe, show us all where the campsite is to be,
And then to the hospital, of which I am eager to see."

"Cornelis and Jan can carry Marinus, Dirck his things, please,
Seebaer and Joannes, bring the... animal, our suffering to ease,
We can set up the third site and prepare our next meal,
Immediately, for Willem's sake, a recovery to deal."

"Throw it on a fire as it is," Hendrik said of the beast,
Wishing to get on with the eating, wishing to feast,
"Why waste your energy cutting away the skin,
And draining the blood; of blood it's already thin?"

Said Ariaen: "There's no need for more blood than necessary,
And it's part of what we call 'farming', Hendrik, it's not scary,
The skin can make boots and a hat, of which we are dire,
I shall not throw good material to the flame of a good fire?"

Hendrik didn't answer, he saw the error of his way, it was clear,
That the others had put more thought into the camps and gear,
He was overlooking many requirements, not to mention,
Of the animal and its by-products, of the general preparation.

"Let's get to work immediately and get Willem something to eat,"
Ariaen then added: "We start trapping soon, requirements to meet,
Let's get moving, for we have camps to set up,
And our food to catch and water to secure, to fill our cup.

Nothing further was said and the men set to duty,
Doing as they should amidst this land of beauty,
For beauty there was if only they should look,
Eyes to see and read, as though lines from a book.

HOLLANDIA NOVA, 1712

By nightfall all had been secured: each and every site,
A small victory, their demise to smite,
All of the survivors came together as darkness fell upon them,
Marinus carried to the main camp, a view worth a gem.

Here he could view the sea,
Easily seen, a feeling of being free,
The meat of the animal had been cut away from the remains,
The ground caked in blood, upon clothing many stains.

The innards thrown aside for the ants and flies to have their way,
For the annoyance to be held back, for them to be held at bay,
The skin was laid upon the ground, for the ants and their raping,
Pegged into place and stretched ready the morning's scraping.

The ants clambered over it and would remove all of the meat,
From the skin, of this leather, of the remains, not being discreet,
And now was the time for a little celebration,
To congratulate one another amidst a common elation.

Each person held a plate of some description, there in the dark,
Whether it be made from wood or a large piece of bark,
Filled with well cooked meat and fat,
Willem wasted no time at all in having his fill of that.

And all around knew that from this day forth,
They would provide special care to Willem, of it he was worth,
To ensure he remained full and spared the more arduous chores,
This was one of their laid down laws.

Wiebbe could only think that the work the boy did earlier,
Contributed to his falling sick, a sheer must to consider,
He knew deep down that he wasn't to blame,
Willem was simply unstoppable, when to work it came.

There was more eating than talking,
Nothing like this meat, none found in all their walking,
Their main staple was shellfish and not always available,
Even though in abundance it was rarely brought to table.

"Do you know something?" said Joannes. "I was thinking,
Thinking that we could build ourselves an oven for cooking,
For the smoking of fish and drying of meat strips,
Jerky to serve us well during our long trips.

"What about the natives?" prodded Dirck. "How do they survive?"
"Don't worry about them," said Jan. "They know how to thrive."
Ariaen: "Which is why we should consider making them friends,
To learn of their ways, and all of their trends."

"It's good to be thinking along the lines of long-term survival,"
Said Hendrik, "but it's not going to aid in a boat's arrival,
We should wait for a boat to appear,
Do all we can to ensure they come near."

Dirck: "And what if one doesn't break our interlude?"
Hendrik: "Don't give me your defeatist attitude,
If a boat doesn't come then we build our own,
Set sail for Batavia, never again to be alone."

HOLLANDIA NOVA, 1712

Dirck added good reasoning to this thought,
"It will do no good unless a launch site is sought,
It's no good building a boat if this can't be secured,
My mind on this matter is bland and cannot be cured."

"But there is a site," said Hendrik. "I heard it mentioned,
Just a few hundred yards away, to the south, there stationed."
Clutching at straws, and why not,
No thought was worthy of rot.

"Take a look, Hendrik," said Seebaer. "It's no good for launching,
We're stuck here and that's all there is to it, on this I'm vouching,
Our only hope is that a ship will be... this way blown,
See our fire, launch a boat: other than that we are on our own."

Silence struck again and the meal was finished,
An appetizing meal, one well wished,
It was then that Ariaen pulled a pipe from within his tattered shirt,
A speech to follow, being rather short and condensed, not curt.

"Do you see what was found by Pieter, a gift from the sea."
"Not much use without tobacco," said Hendrik, on one knee,
"Which I have," said Ariaen as he pulled his tobacco box,
From within his blanket on which he sat, like a crafty fox.

"By God," said Hendrik, "Real tobacco,
Give me some of that and I'll surrender my tomorrow."
"How much is there?" asked Cornelis with a smile,
And this fashion of happy faces did pile and pile.

"Not much," said Ariaen, "I must admit, I have very little store,
But enough to satisfy us each night this week or much more,
If we ration it, I see it lasting a good four week stroke,
But it depends on one thing... who here would like to smoke?"

Voices were raised,
And Ariaen was praised,
A sheer pleasure,
And in reasonable measure.

"We shall have one pipe a night,"
Said Ariane with delight,
"Do you agree?
To feel relaxed and be free?"

All agreed,
Men of single breed,
A tobacco to taste,
Not a single inhale to waste.

And the joyous song of satisfaction went up again,
Now was the time for none to refrain,
The tobacco may not come their way in the future,
And none around to grow or nurture.

Asked Wiebbe: "Shall we consider our order of business?"
"Yes indeed, let's deliberate," said Ariaen, filled with gayness,
Wiebbe: "From our earlier conversations it is clear that a ship,
May very well pass by this way in three days, during its trip."

We should make haste tomorrow and ensure that we are ready,
Ready with a signal fire, of our shipwreck to remedy,
Every able-bodied man should assist,
Help each other, do not resist.

Two persons to remain at the third camp,
To prepare traps, make new, or old to vamp,
A spear would be nice to have,
Thin and flexible, a well struck stave.

We also need a plan of execution,
To attain contact with the native population,
Consider, if you will, a reasonable gift,
We do not wish to cause a rift.

Said Jan: "I don't think that will be a problem,
They will show themselves soon enough; we'll soon see them,
In that I'm quite confident,
Just be free and strident."

"I agree," said Pieter, "but it wouldn't do any harm,
To keep our eyes open, a man to call 'alarm',
Let us try and make the first approach,
A good step towards friendship, not to sit and crouch.

"We need a gift," said Joannes, "something to offer."
"What do you suggest?" asked Hendrik, "for I wouldn't bother."
"I don't know, but something of much worth, something good."
"Food," said Willem. "Everyone desires food."

Said Pieter with a smile: "This is right,
It's as clear as the light,
They have been seen to carry spears,
A current war? None; or so it appears."

"So if not at war,
They must be at tour,
Hunting for food and game,
They too are in need, we are the same."

"We need to dry some meat,
As soon as possible, tendered, well beat,
If we get this done,
Then friendship we have won."

Hendrik: "And how do we know they're friendly?"
"We don't," said Willem, "but we can smile, and act not badly
Make an offering to them, with true conviction,
If they wished to kill us, it would be done, without restriction."

"Maybe," said Hendrik, "maybe not. Only time will tell,
But I tell you all this, right now, in my head, the ringing of bell,
That I care not for these schemes of yours, none at all,
I would much prefer to build a boat, than be speared and fall."

"Hendrik," said Ariaen, "so long as you don't take the wood,
The wood we intend to use on the signal fire, understood?
You can take what you want from the Zuytdorp, all you require,
And don't tempt our combined thoughts, our true desire.

HOLLANDIA NOVA, 1712

Said Hendrik: "And when my boat is ready for the sea,
I shall only take those that make apology,
And those that pay for their place,
With so little time, against time I race."

"Maybe we should make you pay for the tobacco,
How's that Hendrik, a good enough echo?
And the place you keep beside this fire,
The one that you so much admire."

Seeing the error of his way 'again', Hendrik went off, alone to be,
Towards where the cliff top looked out over the calm sea,
The clear of the night growing colder but the wind having died,
Died down to practically nothing, upon the horizon he spied.

The next two days passed fast,
Marinus appeared to be healing, life to last,
Traps made by those at the third campsite were rather petty,
And proved to be ineffective, it was such a pity.

Several large fish were caught from the shoreline platform,
Separated from the ocean where small rock pools did form,
But the ocean was too dangerous to remain next to for too long,
The occasional crashing wave proving to be too strong.

Willem had prevented further attacks by remaining well fed,
Better when compared to the others, guilt on his face easily read,
But he continued to do all he could of the light duties,
Gathering of fuel for fire: '*feed it so that it never dies*'.

Two signal fires were made,
Here men constantly stayed,
Fires some distance apart,
Just to be smart.

Tinder was maintained at the main camp, well dried,
A camp from which they could see far and wide,
The availability of water was also a concern,
Of its procurement they would have to test and learn.

It seemed that everything was in order until the next morning,
The day the Kockenge was expected to appear with little warning,
All were anxious, all were afraid,
All wandered about, near the fires they stayed.

SHIP AHOY

On 11th June, Hendrik was hard at work, a working spree,
Fighting against the thrashing of waves from sea,
Gathering his wood for the building of a boat,
To take him to Batavia, and then he would gloat.

It was simply a matter of time,
Or so he told himself, as over wreckage he did climb,
A matter of time before a ship passed this way,
For him to consider option two, to chase and get in its way.

He maintained a steady watch towards the west,
Doing all he could, his very best,
In the least he provided the other survivors with pieces of wood,
Pieces that didn't serve his purpose, not because he should.

He knew deep down that he was pushing the survivors to hate him,
More and more each passing day, hatred filling to its brim,
But he couldn't help it; it was his way,
So he cast his thoughts aside to work his boat, there to stay.

All felt that the calculations were correct,
That today was the day, one not to neglect,
That a sighting would be made, the Kockenge to be seen,
With sails unfurled to catch the wind, upon the ocean to lean.

But how close the Kockenge was to sail was not clear,
If it was day then it might stay far out to sea, away to steer,
If by night then they would have to rely on a good moon,
Or noise from the ship itself, it could never come too soon.

The bells, bells upon the deck, that's what they would listen for,
The lookout at night would hear any noise, before ship they saw,
Night, however, was a long time off, currently just after noon,
The wait so hard, their need to feel a gratuitous boon.

Dirck took time off from the parties at work,
To check on Marinus and is condition, not to shirk,
Even though Willem had made this one of his sole duties,
Dirck was compelled to assist, one so joyous, not of pities.

For Dirck there was no ulterior motive for his attending this man,
He'd been looking after Marinus since day one, his personal plan,
A promise unto himself, to attend Marinus until fit and well,
Until able to walk upon his own two feet, and for no short spell.

Dirck, a man of faith and great inspiration,
Drew a dirty sleeve across his lips, an action,
A little blood having come from his gum,
He ignored the signature of blood, would remain stum.

As for Wiebbe, he was a man of command, not thick,
Certainly not a healer or comforter of the sick,
To Wiebbe their survival depended on decisions being made,
Not from inaction or from being afraid.

There was himself and Ariaen and Pieter,
The decision makers, nothing sweeter,
Each with the brains to organise and see things through,
Always aiding others and with much to do.

This was a council of three, to whom most would listen,
To heed their suggestions, and always for good reason,
Full of good advice, seemingly wise,
Each an individual, each that always tries.

Pieter had come from a good background,
Where family issues were more important and easily found,
He had a passion for living that his mother had cast,
Put into his mind forever, of conviction to last.

Pieter never reflected upon it much,
Never deliberating, in mind to touch,
He had been rewarded by his parents actions and self-confidence,
To work a solution through and with much patience.

Only held back by Ariaen, it seemed,
Whose very presence was so overpowering, it gleamed,
Ariaen shining through as the decision maker of the group,
Through combined motion of the council, never to stoop.

Ariaen: a man of distinction, a man of healing,
A man of good standing, a man of much feeling,
It was his easy-going nature that made his character,
Drawing an open ear and friendly smile, no actor.

Hendrik knew how to scoff and refuse,
But seldom did this act ever amuse,
Plodding away, gathering wood,
Upon his feet, unsteady he stood.

Just after midday, appeared a freak wave,
Falling heavily upon him, ill-favour it gave,
Bashing him heinously against the rock,
Of vision and consciousness it did knock.

Now washed out to sea,
A sea burial it was to be,
Flesh to be eaten of creatures about,
One man they could all do without.

Seebaer was near the edge of the cliff when the incident occurred,
All he could do was stand there and watch, he hardly stirred,
Despite the fact that the wave was too loud, too large, and fast,
There was nothing one could do, and to the sea Hendrik was cast.

Joannes, Cornelis and Jan were the first to be at Seebaer's side,
Looking down upon Hendrik in that last minute, taken by the tide,
What could be said? Very little,
So far below he looked like a beetle.

How fast the wave took,
How fiercely it shook,
Hendrik drawn mercilessly away,
Rock and wave to flay and flay.

HOLLANDIA NOVA, 1712

Cornelis then saw something on the horizon,
Gave an emotional leap of joyous salvation,
Springing the news upon all around that a ship could be seen,
Nothing more than a little scratch in the distance, of sea a queen.

"I don't see anything," said Jan with hope in his voice,
Almost falling over, waiting to shout, to rejoice,
"It was there," came the exasperation from Cornelis. "I swear,
I swear to God that I saw a ship: for real, not mirage or glare."

"It must be the Kockenge," voiced Ariaen as he came running,
Confused by the sad look of Joannes, when he should be singing,
Compare this to the overcrowded joy of the other three,
"What's wrong, Joannes? A ship... you should be filled with glee."

"Hendrik has gone,
To the hungry sea alone,"
Responded Cornelis: "Leave it, just look for the ship,
Let's not let it slip."

Cornelis: "There it is, there!"
Jan: "I see it, a sight to revere."
"Me too," came a frantic call from Pieter most ripe,
Between sea and sky, the horizon, that fine stripe.

And before long everyone could see the ship in the distance,
Disappearing and then coming to view as it did advance,
The waves obscuring their sight of the ship, now and again,
Here in the sun, no clouds, no rain.

It was sheer jubilation, of great relief it proved,
As though all of their burdens had been removed,
But Ariaen was more sober in thought and gave the command,
To set light to the signal fire, to draw the ship towards land.

His three closest companions set themselves to task,
The signal fire was soon ablaze, uplifting their mask,
Unveiling their position for the world to see,
For the world this minute was a ship to set them free.

Pieter had alerted the others to the rear of the approaching vessel,
Before returning to stand by Ariaen, his emotions in a wrestle,
Pieter saw the expression, no smile or grin so painted,
Just a simple, sober look, rather grey and slated.

"What is it, Ariaen," asked Pieter. "Have you seen a ghost?"
"If we can see the ship, then the ship can see the coast,"
He answered nonchalantly, "which means that they will turn,
Turn to the north at any minute: in hell we're to burn."

"I'm sure as sure can be, there will be many eyes cast this way,
But fire not seen, and in our direction, the ship will not stay,
Men will be resting below deck or busy upon it, and rather keen,
Keen to be on their way, For I'm an experienced sailor, not green."

"They have no navigational reference for this region,
That will confirm their position,
So the lookout will have his eyes cast to the north,
Not to the east, no favour for us brought forth."

HOLLANDIA NOVA, 1712

"I know: they seek the bay, possibly fifty miles to the north,
The best and only real navigation point they have of any worth,
Aye, I see the look in your eye, but I've taken many notes,
Scribed upon my mind is the layout of the stars, dots and quotes."

"You know as much as I of our predicament,
Of the ship; with the fire this moment,
The way men work on the sea is one of question upon question,
Confirmation needed on their position, not of fire to mention."

"Our only hope lays in the reality that the smoke might ignite,
Ignite suspicion when they reach Batavia, consider our plight,
They will then learn of our disappearance,
Consider this signal, a signal of our cumbrance."

Ariaen looked at the others, some having stopped in their tracks,
"Light the second fire, immediately; let burn these stacks,
Our only hope: that they will see our fire, to later be in the know,
Once in Batavia on learning of our failure to show."

And the men worked as they had never worked before,
Setting fire to the second, running for more wood they tore,
"If the natives didn't know of us," said Joannes, "they do now."
And to the fate of the future they must bow.

And that was the first and last ship they saw,
15th: Oostersteyn, 24th: Zuyderbeeck, 25th: Belvliet, and more,
29th: Popkensburg, 5th July: Corsloot and Oude Zyp: no sight,
All had bypassed them unseen, either by day or by night.

Too far out to be seen or passing further to the north of land,
Salvation not to come their way, no shaking of hand,
And so the signal fires sat at the ready until employed elsewhere,
Wood needed for their campsite, to survive a life so unfair.

PREPARATIONS

12th July: They all sat around the campfire of the main site,
These days, the beginning of winter, rain scarce, water rites tight,
They learnt to set traps for the smaller animals of land,
And tested morsels of carcasses found, being far from grand.

Beetles and small grubs, occasionally mixed in with other sources,
But this was always accompanied by a sour look upon faces,
Willem had suffered from minor attacks of Porphyria Variegate,
But never serious enough to see his basic health deteriorate.

At any time that an attack arrived out of the blue,
The men would give up most of their stew,
In order for Willem to gain a few extra days of nourishment,
An act of brotherly love, a gift of care, not of payment.

Marinus was forever on the recovery, health so slow to gain,
His ribs had seemingly healed but there was still plenty of pain,
He often joked about his arm and restriction,
The trouble with wiping his backside, and then the ablution.

"And you, Jan?" asked Pieter, "What are you contemplating?"
"Oh; nothing, really. I was thinking of these shoes and their aging,
They're near the end of their life," and Jan looked down,
Looked upon the big toes of both feet, dreary and brown.

They were showing through breaks in the leather,
exposed to the torments of the cold, the bad weather,
"I nearly burnt my feet the other night,
Toes bare to the flames of our fire so bright."

"Wrap another blanket," suggested Seebaer, "around your feet,
You'll do even better if you keep them dry: even an old sheet."
A few of the men looked around; they didn't have a spare blanket,
No spare shoes, clothes, shirt or jacket.

"I was thinking of getting shoes made from one of those furs,
Like you and Marinus," said Jan to Seebaer, "or like Pieter's."
"You can have the next one," said Ariaen, most sincere,
The truth being that all were in need most dear.

"What other needs do we currently have?" asked Ariaen of all,
"Apart from food, water; clothing and shoes; for summer to fall?"
Said Wiebbe, thinking of Dirck: "We need something for scurvy,
And I think we need it in a hurry."

Dirck did avail himself to the aid of all other,
Having neglected the effects: "I saw the way he did suffer."
They all knew that Wiebbe was right,
They needed good nourishment, scurvy to fight.

Roots were needed, some form of edible fruit,
This was their goal, on top of their list, this constant pursuit,
But how to secure this need?
Anything would do, even a seed.

"Dirck was a good man," voiced Marinus as he rubbed his arm,
The pain showing upon his face, a constant alarm,
The joining of the two bones not being as perfect as it should,
"I feel a little responsible for his death," as any man would.

"Don't," said Wiebbe. "He wouldn't want you to think that."
"He served me well," added Marinus, "beside me he sat."
"He served us all well," said Ariaen. "It wasn't your fault he died,
He died of scurvy. He hid the truth of his condition: he lied."

Cornelis: "He was transferred to the Zuytdorp from another ship,
He'd only be ashore one or two days, full of friendship,
No time at all to fill up on fruit or cabbage,
Hardly touching any fruit during his entire passage.

"Ah, cabbage," said Wiebbe, wishing to forget Dirck's death,
The way he suffered, his drawing of last breath,
Scurvy had taken its toll on his body, killing him over time,
"That's what we need now, something green, something sublime."

"There's nothing here but scrub," said Seebaer. "Nothing to eat."
Pieter looked at the others, "We need natives to meet,
For our survival it's the only way,
For we deteriorate more every day."

Ariaen: "I think it's time we voted on the matter,
Who's in favour of making contact, sooner than later,
Raise your hand,
Make your stand."

Seebaer: "But one thing must be said,
We must wait until the end of August, and then put rescue to bed,
If no ship has returned by then, then we should proceed,
Upon this point of fact we must all be agreed."

"NO," said Cornelis. "That's too late. We need to act now,
Not purposely wait for a boat, a solid raft, or a flimsy scow,
We can still remain here, until the beginning of summer,
But not rely, or waste effort, on this former."

"A vessel of the VOC is not going to come,
I'm being realistic, not glum,
Scurvy is treacherous to us all and Willem is suffering,
We need help now, for our health requires buffering."

"Good," said Ariaen. "So let's consider it agreed,
We'll remain here until summer, but must fulfill our need,
Joannes said: "And what are we going to barter?
Why would the natives help us? You believe them not smarter?"

"Well... we have nothing, really," answered Pieter in truth,
"Maybe some coins from the wreck, but I am no sleuth,
I believe we are smarter than the natives: we can build a boat,
But they know this land, they have it by the throat.

Concluded Ariaen: "All we can do is show good intention,
and hope for the best, and show no aggression,
I doubt for a minute they're aggressive,
Or we'd be dead already, sitting here most passive."

"He's right," defended Marinus. "Jan saw one,
Just a few days ago, probably alone."
"Yes," admitting Jan, reminding all of the encounter,
"And all he could do was stand there, to loiter."

"Watching me, clad in a single fur. I don't like them,
That's the conclusion I've come to, that's my problem,
It was raining and he'd come quite close but soon walked off,
He wasn't afraid, either. Just disappeared, as though to scoff."

"They're not animals," said Ariaen, "I'm sure he meant no insult,
They must've lived on this land for many years, achieved result,
They know the way of the land, something you may have forgot,
They know what is good to eat and what is not."

"We'll die if we stay here and do nothing,
I'm growing tired of waiting: within I'm seething,
We need to act,
That is a fact."

Seebaer volunteered: "Let me take a small party into the east,
Let me do this for all of us, bring to heel this unknown beast,
Bring to our lips a grand feast,
This the least I can do, the least."

Ariaen was silent for a moment and then nodded his head,
"Very well. Take as much water as you can carry, blanket for bed,
And eat well before you depart,
And always be ready, always be smart."

Seebaer: "We'll be gone just a few days, no more than four,
It'll only be a very short tour,
And this time we'll want to be seen,
To meet them we'll remain steadfast and keen."

"Very well," agreed Ariaen as he reached for his tobacco and pipe,
"I have enough for one more smoke," his mouth he did wipe,
"A large portion to do us all, the last,
Let's finish this tobacco, a thing of our past."

Seebaer, Cornelis and Jan all smiled, filled with elation,
Marinus then turned to Seebaer with a question,
"Who do you want to take along?"
"Cornelis, Jan and Joannes; together we're strong."

Marinus took the fur shoes from his feet and handed them to Jan,
"Take these with you: of them I am no fan."
"Thank you, Marinus, you liar," came the sincere gratitude,
Accepted them most happily, for to refuse would be rude.

Marinus managed to get Jan's old shoes on his feet with trouble,
Felt immediately the discomfort, understood why Jan did stumble,
No man could walk properly in these,
Of fine workmanship you could no longer tease.

But smile they did,
True feelings hid,
Marinus did the right thing,
Jan now happy, his feet could sing.

OF CANNIBAL OR NATIVE

The group departed after having eaten enough to sink a ship,
Eating more than their usual share before commencing their trip,
They carried a receptacle each, differing in purpose and shape,
To portage their water, all that they could scrape.

They each carried a blanket,
A little sail cloth: a sort of jacket,
Able to be wrapped around them,
Or as a shelter, weather to hem.

They also had several pieces of rope,
Such commodity always gave hope,
For something always needed to be tied,
On it they most heavily relied.

They hadn't travelled far when they saw a familiar sight,
A kangaroo hopping away, scurrying off in fright,
Followed shortly thereafter by two more, Jan did smile and laugh,
And within a few more minutes an emu crossed their path.

They had never spoken of trying to catch an emu for food,
Too large and fast to chase, unless a young brood,
Did they taste similar to chicken?
Were they disease stricken?

Three quarters of the day had fallen before their first encounter,
An old fireplace, with sign of there being a shelter,
A hearth which had been abandoned long ago,
A sparse stick, or spear, but not ready to throw.

There were several bones, white and dry,
No way of knowing if it was eaten or did it simply die,
Cleaned well by the ants and the weather,
Or stripped bear with teeth and temper.

But on they went,
Their energy spent,
Two more hours before the sun said good night,
Goodbye to the day's last light.

But they exert themselves upon the current task,
Carrying their gear, and water in varied cask,
To continue on and do, no need of questions to ask,
No desire to stop in the late of day's sun to bask.

And then Joannes did make complaint,
Feeling on the edge of a faint,
"I don't know if I can continue like this for much longer,
I have no energy, I am not young and stronger.

At 37 years of age he was not that old,
But he was reasonable intelligent and bold,
Showed the signs of being worse for ware,
Amidst friends as they did stare.

HOLLANDIA NOVA, 1712

Seebaer stopped dead in his tracks,
Hearing Joannes, seeing the energy he lacks,
Just behind Cornelis, who, being the youngest of the group,
Had pressed a little ahead, to look and snoop.

"Cornelis; wait," stammered Seebaer, turning to the other two,
"Let's camp here for the night; I think today we're through,
We've done enough, we should try and find something to eat,
Erect a shelter, prepare for slumber, some rest to greet.

Cornelis said not a word, moved back to join his comrades,
They were tired and weary, not natives, not nomads,
Each fell upon the hard floor of the sandplains,
Each sighing with relief, feeling those numerous pains.

Asked Jan of the others: "Doesn't this place ever change?"
"You came this way," said Cornelis of Jan. "To me it's strange."
"What do you see?" questioned Jan of his friend. "It's the same,
No matter where you go, a land you could never tame."

Jan: "Sure, the scenery changes a little, but its not arable,
For the most part it is dry and uninhabitable."
Joannes: "Hence why it's important to make good with natives,"
"No good can come of the natives," said Jan, as he freely gives.

"Then why are you here?" asked Joannes most rightly,
"Here or there, what does it matter?" replied Jan most sprightly,
"The inevitable will happen sooner or later,
We'll all die on this damn land, on that you can wager."

"Don't say that, Jan," insisted Seebaer. "There is always hope."
"Hope didn't help Harmen," continued Jan, unable to cope,
"Where there is God, there is hope," said Seebaer of belief,
Hoping the comment would provide a little relief.

"Yes, well," said Jan, his eyes upturned just a bit,
"If ever there was a Garden of Eden, this is not it,
God has nothing good in store,
Even if we obey his every law."

"We're alive," said Seebaer, "Even if not strong."
Asked Jan: "But for how long?"
Cornelis: "I'll try and find something to eat, walk out my cramp,
I'll take a look around whilst you set up camp."

"Joannes can come with me."
"I don't have the energy, can't you see?"
But Cornelis scoffed, insisted he attend,
Just a relaxing walk, his spirits to mend.

And quite a while later, the dark sky commenced its move,
And a howling in the distance, of which not to approve,
An howl shaking both Seebaer and Jan awake, sleep unexpected,
They'd fallen asleep shortly after the shelter had been erected.

"That's close," said Jan, quite afraid,
"Too close," agreed Seebaer from where he laid,
"Where are Cornelis and Joannes, do you know?
They've been gone a long time: why don't they show?"

HOLLANDIA NOVA, 1712

Jan looked around as fear took a grip,
He knew that no good would come of this trip,
"CORNELIS... JOANNES," yelled Jan with all his might,
Several dozen birds in a nearby tree taking flight.

The sky was beautiful, a band of orange spanning the horizon,
From north to south. "CORNELIS... JOANNES." Going, the sun,
They both listened, nothing, heard, no reply, no howling dog,
Nothing: no overture of birds, insects, no scurrying lizard or frog.

Just a few seconds,
Eerie, and fear beckons,
The unknown was scary,
Time to be weary.

Seebaer: "That damn beast isn't far. I saw one the other week,
A great reddish-brown animal looking at me: such a mean streak,
Watching whilst I cooked upon the campfire a meal,
I guess he wanted to come in, an attempt to steal."

"Are they big?" asked Jan, with his fear in touch,
"Big enough," answered Seebaer. "It doesn't take much,
Even a small wolf can bring down a man or two,
CORNELIS... JOANNES, WHERE ARE YOU."

Seebaer stood silently and listened with his entire might,
"They aren't answering: out of range; out of sight,
We'll have to get some rest, take turns maintaining watch,
A task we need to do well, not one to botch."

Seebaer looked into Jan's eyes. "We'll get some firewood,
And see if that tinderbox Ariaen gave us is any good."
"I only hope we live to be able to give it back."
"Don't talk like that, Jan. No dog is going to attack."

Further away: Asked Cornelis: "Did you hear that; so eerie."
"It's just a dog," said Joannes. "It's far away, don't worry,
I can hardly hear it, for the most,
I'm more concerned about being lost."

Insisted Cornelis: "We're not lost; I've told you before,
All we need to do is to turn west and head towards shore."
"That's over a day's walk," Joannes pointed out,
"And here we are, leisurely walking about."

Cornelis: "We'll have to stay here tonight,
Find our way back with the morning's first light."
"You know something strange?" said Joannes. "I feel tired,
And yet I don't think I can sleep. I feel alive: inspired."

"The exhaustion I feel right now is the worst I've felt,
But the thoughts in my head are being dealt and dealt,
It's as though I see a hundred images all at once,
Each having something to say, something to announce."

"Yes, well; We'll just sit and talk awhile, listen to the land,"
Said Cornelis, "see what it has to say, see where we stand."
"Yes, I think..." and Joannes' jaw dropped sharply as he looked,
Up and beyond where Cornelis was seated, his vision hooked.

HOLLANDIA NOVA, 1712

Cornelis had a look of bewilderment and froze there on the spot,
His eyes darted from left to right, but to look back he dared not,
"Joannes; there's someone behind me, isn't there?"
"Yes," replied Joannes, as he continued to stare.

"Please don't move quickly,
Do nothing at all too abruptly,
For there are six natives standing so near,
And each is carrying a sharp-pointed spear."

"Looking for food," Cornelis said blankly and praying,
Unable to think of anything to say that was worth saying,
"Probably," answered Joannes, thinking of their immediate fate,
And I think we're it, unable to do much, and in a bad state."

LIVE OR DIE

For both Jan and Seebaer the night had been long,
Each having taken turns to stay awake, until mornings first song,
Concerned for the welfare of their comrades and their own,
The fire remained reasonably well lit, upon it wood thrown.

The two men tried effortlessly one more time to call upon friend,
To call them home: huh, home; was this to be their trend,
And after another two hours of sitting and waiting,
They decided to return to the cliff, no need for debating.

It was quite obvious to them both that the other two would show,
Would come of their senses, head for the coast they did know,
Jan quickly doused the fire, the last embers smothered,
Considering now the much ground that needed to be covered.

The sun was hotter today than any over the past week,
And of this neither man needed to speak,
The land around them seemed worthless beyond all contemplation,
The ground unable to offer a single ounce of good traction.

But what the eye failed to see was a land of great offering,
Many gifts going unnoticed by the Dutch amidst scoffing,
For much food and water was available, if only they looked,
The land they walked filled to the brim of much to be cooked.

HOLLANDIA NOVA, 1712

Again the day grew long and commenced to draw to a close,
But not before the two men could hear a noise as it rose,
The familiar sound of ocean breaking its back against platform,
Of where the Zuytdorp was hit so harshly by storm.

They literally staggered in, Ariaen and Pieter the first upon feet,
To provide assistance as needed, there to readily greet,
A crackling fire, warm and inviting,
To be here was both sad and exciting.

Willem scrambled to help but was quickly asked for aid,
To quickly throw some food upon the fire, a meal to be made,
Marinus dragged out a water container for the men to drink,
And then came the questions, with no time left to think.

"Where's Cornelis and Joannes?" asked Ariaen most concerned,
"They're gone," replied Seebaer, the onlookers had now learned,
News gifted through cracked lips, barely audible but understood,
No hiding of the truth, no speaking of falsehood.

"Let them sit and drink," urged Pieter, "They're thirsty."
"You're right," agreed Ariaen, "Their throats must be dusty."
And then a little silence, no further question to ask,
Until they had eaten and drank, and were ready for such a task.

Several mouthfuls of water later and after a deep breath,
Seebaer broke the news all were eager to hear, but not of death,
"They're lost; they wandered off for just a few minutes."
Said Ariaen: "tell us all, I'm sure you have no secrets."

Said Seebaer: "Last night: we'd been walking almost all day,
Needed somewhere to bed down, somewhere to stay,
We'd gone much further than Jan and Harmen had gone,
Other than exhaustion, nothing seemed to be going wrong."

"With some time before nightfall, Cornelis took Joannes away,
To search the area for water and food, without further delay,
That night I took first watch, and when I woke,
All I saw was Jan and our fire, and a little smoke."

"We called to them forever, but to no avail,
That is about the length of our tale,
We had to return." He kicked out at the dirt. "This sodden place,
It's like hell on earth. There's none worse, a land with no face."

Pieter then broke the silence, "Do you think they're dead?"
"Time will tell," said Ariaen soberly. "Let's not fill our head,
With false notions or guesses: let's just consider them as living,
But as Seebaer has said, this place is unforgiving."

"Maybe it is, maybe it's not," said Pieter, "but it can be tamed."
"No," said Seebaer, "it will be taming us, of this I am ashamed."
"Seebaer is right," said Wiebbe, sucking his lips into his mouth,
"We have to try to live with the land, or we sink and go south."

"That's what we're doing," said Jan, "trying to live with the land."
"No," said Wiebbe, "We've been surviving, trying to stand,
But not melding with it. We have to become one, or its over,
Be truly a part of Hollandia Nova."

"To be whipped by land!" said Seebaer. "To become a savage?"
"Your so-called savages have lived on this land, they manage,
For longer than we've been sailing past it, here they've lived,
For hundreds of years, they've learnt, they've thrived."

"No," disagreed Marinus. "Where are their houses, achievements,
Where are the everyday signs of their accomplishments?"
"Maybe the land doesn't permit it," answered Pieter most sheer,
Wiebbe: "I agree.... Time for us to be the true pioneer."

Said Seebaer: "That's what we've been trying,
And all that's happened is we keep on dying,
We've been south, north and east, and nothing has been found,
Limited, yes, but we've made that asserted effort, one to astound."

"It's not enough," said Wiebbe. "We have to do more than swoon,
We have to make contact with the natives and soon,
When winter has gone and the last of storm has come to pass,
The days will become hot upon this land of little to no grass."

"It will be like walking across the face of an anvil,
Look around you; all of you; a sheer hell,
This land doesn't know anything but the harsh realities of life,
And we must learn to live with all of its strife."

I've seen other lands which have succumb to the torments of heat,
Heat upon heat, upon heat; so hot it burns through the sole of feet,
I have seen other lands which have been spared no remorse,
A sun so hot it melts the mind of man; and in minutes of course.

But I have never seen a land like this, beaten harsh by a hot rod,
The ground so savagely treated by the open hand of God,
Where no Dutch flower can blossom nor a bee gather nectar,
We must prepare for the worst, to stand, not lay upon stretcher."

"What makes you think," scoffed Seebaer. "We won't die,
Right on this spot, beneath a heinous sun and cursed land to fry?"
Said Wiebbe: "Because I'll always hold onto the hope within me,"
"If I lose that, I lose all; even the right to die right: don't you see."

DEPARTURE

18th July: The weather remained rather moderate,
And over the coming the days a little rain at slow rate,
Not enough to fill the gullies with running water,
But enough to cause some misery and moods to alter.

Willem and Pieter stood before the third camp laid,
And secured into place, upon a tree, an arrow they had made,
It consisted of a shaft with two shorter pieces of wood attached,
To resemble a pointer, a bread crumb, and so niched.

"Do you think it will work, Pieter?" asked Willem unsure,
"I don't know, Willem," he said in return. "But it's a good lure,
Any man could see this from reasonable distance, but honestly,
I don't think we'll ever see them again, and that sounds ghastly."

"But if Cornelis and Joannes do come back this way,
They're sure to check each of the camp sites without delay,
Searching each for materials they might be able to use,
When they see this marker, they'll know the direction to choose."

Pieter helped with the final knot and he stepped back,
Of distinctness the sigh did not lack,
They hence turned to join the others, a timely arrival,
All manner of items to go with them in their forage for survival.

Each carried his own blanket and anything else on which to think,
Every second man a container for the porting of water to drink,
A few others carried one of the three knives or makeshift spears,
These weapons themselves helped shave off their fears.

They stood around the burnt out fire, a slight glow emanating,
Hotter embers deep within the mound of charcoal venting,
"We should have made a note for them from the charcoal,"
Said Marinus allowed, their despicable situation taking its toll.

Said Pieter: "The arrow that Willem made is a good enough sign,
If they come then they will see, and then all will be fine."
Marinus said: "I just wish we could have done more for them,"
As he reflected upon the realities of predicament and problem.

"Maybe we should wait a little longer; just a few days more."
Said Ariaen. "Our decision is made, survival we cannot ignore,
We can't keep holding onto false hope."
"You're right," agreed Marinus. "Let's go; let's not mope."

They commenced their journey, having committed no crime,
Their eyes falling upon their home for the final time,
A little guilt within each saying they had done wrong,
To continue with their singing, to continue with the song.

A seemingly sad farewell to a place they had come to know,
And now they were leaving it behind, their feelings low,
Northward to search for something more rewarding,
Ariaen led the way, followed by Pieter and Willem, now walking.

HOLLANDIA NOVA, 1712

"Come on, Marinus," urged Wiebbe, "time to go."
Marinus tagged on, following the others, off into tomorrow,
Seebaer and Jan carried several poles for erecting a shelter,
Should the need arise when they stopped much later.

A temporary solution to aid in protection should it rain,
Something good to ward off the cold and the pain,
It would do them until something more permanent could be found,
Something more sturdy, more solid, much more sound.

Wiebbe took up the rear of the file, holding to chest his worries,
Glancing one final time over the site which had many memories,
Most of which he looked forward to forgetting,
Now to the future, where he hoped to find plenty of growing.

He said his goodbye to the site,
As though a last rite,
A camp he saw mature,
For laziness a sure cure,

DELIBERATION

They'd not been gone long, when Marinus stopped in his tracks,
"What is it, Marinus?" asked Seebaer, trying to see any cracks,
The others now stopping to see what mattered,
What was the cause for their trek to be shattered.

Marinus announced to all so that there was no mistake,
About what he was about to do, of an errand to make,
"I have to go back. We left no water for the other two."
"There's water in the rock hole," said Pieter, "They'll do."

"No," said Marinus. "That's almost gone,
If we leave them nothing… that's just wrong."
He looked to the ground and made his final decision,
"I'm going back to leave my water, in a good position."

"Marinus;" said Ariaen, "the animals will get at it."
"I'll hang it from a tree," insisted Marinus, quick with wit,
"You're wasting your time," said Jan, "and ours: all the more."
Marinus was silent, shaking a few of them to the core.

"Don't wait for me. I'll catch up: there's plenty of daylight,
All I have to do is follow the cliff;" said he; "right?"
"That's right," said Wiebbe, "the cliff and the sound,
You can also follow our footprints on the ground."

"Good; then you all go and I'll catch up soon enough."
"Are you sure?" asked Pieter, "With your pain it may be rough."
"Yes; very sure. You all go on ahead: a short stretch of the leg."
"Take someone with you," suggested Pieter, not wishing to beg.

Willem volunteered: "I'll go,"
Said Pieter: "You don't have the energy; no."
"No," assured Marinus. "Please; I'll go alone,
I need to do this for our friends, it must be done."

A silent nod was all that was needed,
Marinus, back to camp, he headed,
To hang his water from the tree,
For his dear friends to openly see.

Marinus stepped out upon the worn track,
Which lead, to the second campsite, all the way back,
And happy he was, for finding his way was easy,
As too was he thankful that at last he was busy.

The slight pain he felt in his arm and chest were shrugged off,
Now so used to it he could only scoff,
It being nothing more than a small hindrance,
To him it made little difference.

He stepped out onto the nakedness of the site and was confronted,
By sheer surprise, four sets of gnarled teeth well noted,
A viciousness he'd never seen or encountered before,
A small pack of dogs to lay down the law.

A deep throaty growl then surfaced from the first,
Of all before him he appeared the largest: the worst,
They commenced to encircle him, preventing any escape,
Smelling his flesh, waiting to tear, bite, scratch and scrape.

Dingoes; massive and hungry for easy prey,
They could sense the inabilities of Marinus, could do as they may,
They could smell the water and above all his weakness, his fear,
Smaller than a fully-grown, male kangaroo, he did appear.

For the dingo it was an opportunity, a matter of survival,
Marinus was simply an easy target, frail, wounded, unable,
Unable to control his fear, or to ward off a savage beating,
The dingoes would go to work upon him and end their meeting.

The animals closed in upon their game,
And then the attack came,
From the rear,
Viciousness at full gear.

The cry that filled the air was heinous to say the least,
The worst death cry that the men had heard from man or beast,
All they could do was stop, turn and stare, everyone the same,
looking out in the direction from whence the cries came.

And it soon fell silent, the screaming having come to an end,
"We should go back," urged Willem, "and help our friend."
"NO!" said Jan. "It was his own foolish decision,
He should have been careful, had a clearer vision.

"You're wrong, Jan. It wasn't foolish to want to help a friend,
No more foolish than it is for Willem to go and attend,
Attend to Marinus..." said Ariaen. "But it's now too late,
Marinus has met his end, of him you need not berate."

"Those damn savages," spat Jan. "They are simply no good,
We should kill them before they kill us all; we should; I would."
"He's right," said Seebaer. "On the savages you cannot rely,
We can't befriend them. They're heinous, of this I can't deny."

"You see," said Jan. "They're cannibals, every last one."
"He's right," said Pieter. "Why kill Marinus, he, weak and alone?"
"Maybe it wasn't the natives," advised Wiebbe. "You don't know,
Maybe it was a snake or something. We should go back; let's go."

"One of those dogs," suggested Ariaen. "And Willem, you stay."
"No. No, no, no; that's no dog," insisted Seebaer. "Not today,
A scream like that? And no snake either,
The savages were waiting, have been watching forever."

"They see us, they know where we are; they see,
But we've seen them before, haven't we?"
"Yes," said Jan. "They've had plenty of time to approach,
So why haven't they? Because our lives they poach."

Said Ariaen: "Maybe they're scared."
"No; they're not scared; but of hatred they've bared,
No man would wait as long as this before coming forward,
If his intentions were honourable; unless a coward."

Asked Ariaen: "Then what do you suggest?"
"Kill them," said Jan. "Without rest,
"Don't be stupid," spat Wiebbe. "We're too few."
"Only one solution exists," insisted Ariaen. "A rescue."

"And if rescue doesn't come?" asked Seebaer upfront,
"We stay clear of the natives, avoid them, never to confront,
We find somewhere to sustain us, a place to survive,
Find some savages that won't kill us, somewhere to stay alive."

"I don't trust you," said Seebaer. "I want a new leader,
Someone more readily able to see to our needs, someone bolder."
Ariaen and Pieter remained calm, standing rigid,
A call for a change in leadership could not be forbid.

"Listen to me," said Ariaen, unforgiving,
Of his post he was not leaving,
"If you wish new leadership, of our structure to quit,
Then you go off by yourself and try to find it."

"Pieter, Willem and Wiebbe are coming with me, with me to stay,
And Jan, are you with me or Seebaer, what do you say?"
Jan could see the manipulation of the talk,
As easily as Seebaer and he could walk.

"Stop," said Seebaer holding up his palms in defeat, in disgrace,
A funny little smirk upon his face,
"I see where this is leading,
Do you think me of foolish breeding?"

HOLLANDIA NOVA, 1712

"I'll stay with you, Ariaen. I'll not cause any further trouble,
But remember this: we are not pieces of discarded rubble,
We all have the right to voice our own opinion,
Whether or not there is any good reason."

Ariaen: "So long as it's an opinion,
And not a confrontation,
Nor mutiny or war,
I'll say no more."

"You are free to voice all you want,
You are free to… politically confront,
I suggest we continue on our way,
Remain on our bearing north and not stray."

ANCESTORS

20th July: The sun broke the horizon when an aboriginal fell,
Fell upon the scene of Marinus ripped to shreds, no more to tell,
All of the signs were there; it was a pack of dingoes for sure,
And they'd made short work of Marinus, a semblance of gore.

He gazed around with his spear in hand and looked upon the tree,
A pointer made from wood, a curious device, easy to see,
Its reason for being did initially elude him,
And then it hit him hard, firm and trim.

The white spirits had left a message, both primitive and simple,
Through the Malgana territory and towards the Yinggarda people,
That was the direction they intended to go, to greet and interact,
That's why the spirits - these people - had failed to make contact.

But what of the other two spirits that had been found so recently?
Barega was his name, and he thought this quite discreetly,
He was an aboriginal of the Malgana people, of the Wayle tribe,
He was a tall fellow of handsome features, full of good vibe.

He had deep creases within his face displaying great character,
He stood naked with a small shield, and a spear to shatter,
Shatter the lives of animals for food, to cook on fire, or smoulder,
And had a small cloak of fur which he carried round his shoulder.

HOLLANDIA NOVA, 1712

The cloak was a gift from the Nanda to the south,
The people of that vicinity who offered proposal by mouth,
With an interest in a marital corroboree in the near future,
For the tribes to commit, to be friendly, to give aid, to nurture.

He would provide this news to his elders, make them understand,
His tribe had heard, that white spirits had fallen upon the land,
Making visit upon them from across the ocean so vast,
It was all new to him, these people, their ships and mast.

Many times were ships seen passing them by and at full sail,
And in all that time it remained mystifying, it never did fail,
Such a strange unknown site; but now they knew instead,
The ships floated upon the water carried the spirits of the dead.

But something more troubled him, and confusion then rose,
How could a spirit of the dead be killed by a pack of dingoes,
If these visitors were indeed ancestors of the living,
Then surely they'd not be able to perish, undergo such misgiving.

Barega saw the obvious, a corpse where spirit was released,
Blood was everywhere, this man was living, but now deceased,
Flesh and tendons bare to the world as though free,
This wasn't the spirit of the dead; how could it be?

WHITE MAN'S CORROBOREE

The group of survivors continued reluctantly on their way,
To the north, pressing on in their misery, searching for a bay,
Seebaer could not restrain himself any longer,
He now feeling weaker, but of spirit much stronger.

The episode of death two days before was playing on his mind,
"Stop; wait," said he from the rear, the march coming to a grind,
Said Wiebbe: "We need to keep walking,"
"Stop, I say," repeated Seebaer. "Listen to me, I'm talking."

"All of you. Don't you see," and the others gathered round,
"They're killing us off, of their morals none can be found,
They intend to eat us, right down to the bone,
To cook us on fires, hot rocks, and hot stone."

"That's ridiculous," urged Pieter. "Why would they do that?"
"Why walk naked in the heat or cold?" said Seebaer as he spat,
"I don't know their ways but the intention is quite clear."
He turned to Jan. "You heard Marinus scream; his sheer fear?"

"Aye," said Jan, "The most terrible scream I've ever heard."
"Seebaer, you're ridiculous," said Wiebbe, "quite weird,
But presume you're correct about them, through and through,
What would you suggest, what would you have us do?"

HOLLANDIA NOVA, 1712

"We must fight," he said, "stand and deliver."
"Seebaer," said Pieter calmly. "We have rope, a shelter,
Blankets, a little water and three knives,
No comfort, no water or food, no wives."

Seebaer: "I don't know, but we must think of something."
Ariaen: "We're going to head north, of more... there's nothing,
Return to the camp if you like, and be lost forever,
Or come with us, where lies your true tether."

Seebaer was silent for a moment but again came to his senses,
Realising that his petty feud was useless against this herd of asses,
That Wiebbe, Pieter and Willem would not do anything to disrupt,
The friendship between them and Ariaen, being politically corrupt.

"Okay, I'll take my orders as you believe I should."
Said Seebaer sarcastically: if only he could,
"No one's pressing you to take orders, Seebaer, and none given,
Decision rests with the majority, and always with good reason.

So they continued on their way with little further said,
Until only a few short hours later, midday to be read,
For the position of the sun, warned all that it was noon,
Time for a rest, and not a time too soon.

There was a frame of sticks, long and fat,
Upon which a fur of wombat hide sat,
They moved this without question,
What was found was no cause for tension.

For here they found what appeared to be a deep well,
Dug into the ground, into darkness it fell,
A poorly constructed hole in which to catch water,
It's precious worth quick to register.

The group fell upon it with excitement, filled with hope,
Quick to tie an empty water container to length of rope,
Lowering it into the seemingly shallow well,
To replenish their core and to rest a spell.

They each and everyone had their fill,
To harness water in this way you needed skill,
Wiebbe: "How do you suppose this came to exist?"
"Maybe shipwrecked sailors; they're survival to assist."

Seebaer stood up then, "I have to go for a walk... to relieve myself,
I have pains. Jan; are you coming, for protection; my health."
And the two walked off towards where the cliff did stand,
To take time from the group, from the unfriendly band.

Ariaen waited for the two men to disappear from view and earshot,
"Let them be. Don't argue, please. I've had enough of his rot."
"I'm not like you," said Wiebbe. "I can't put up with the poison,
You take it well, amidst his pessimism, and without good reason."

"I wish I were more like you. But I must say this, I can be—."
"Look," interrupted Wiebbe, "don't be startled. There... see."
The group of four looked up and saw six aboriginal men,
Not more than eighty feet away, a view to possibly condemn.

Four of them wore what appeared to be a small cloak,
Each a waist belt and arm bands, doing nothing to provoke,
Three of the men carried several small lizards from their belt,
Kills secured by the weapons they carried, or so each felt.

Several of them carried a spear,
[Boomerangs] And bent sticks did appear,
A thick stick with a stone head attached with human hair,
A small hatchet, accompanied by no friendly or unfriendly stare.

One of the natives then looked to the others, this was clear,
Their eyes fixed upon the survivors, with no stance of fear,
Several nods of the head were then seen as one stepped forward,
A graceful movement, seemingly at ease, not awkward.

"Show no fear," said Adriane. "Smile, be friendly; move slow."
"*Are these the spirits?*" asked Kulan, "*the ones you know?*"
"*They look...*" began Narrah, "*like the others from the bush?*"
"What did they say?" whispered Pieter, Wiebbe issuing a 'hush'.

The six natives fell silent and looked again,
Kulan stepped forward, not wishing to refrain,
And made his approach in peace with an offering,
A small goanna now in his right hand, of friendship to bring.

"*Take this food; it's good,*" said Kulan. "*We have ample,
The yellow fat of the goanna is a delicacy amongst my people.*"
"He's offering you something," said Pieter of the obvious.
"Quickly, take it or he'll be offended; or become furious."

Wiebbe took the food and smiled, bowing slightly,
"Thank you," he said, most rightly,
Kulan stepped back and turned, happy in what he did do,
"You see; they're happy to receive it, just like the other two."

Said Nioka: *"They look at it in such a strange way,*
And I understand so little of their ancestry this day,
Show him you killed it, a gift for him and his people,"
But make it short, pure and simple."

It was unknown to the survivors that dance was a formality,
Of communication in many ways, a great stability,
This was a corroboree and involved much movement,
Imitating animals and actions, of past or present moment.

Some represented hunters, or bouts of conflict,
None meant to ridicule, some made up and could not be predict,
All movement told a story and many new ones were developed,
To be told and recorded for all time in minds embedded.

The history of the tribe passed from one generation to the next,
Most accompanied by music, none scored via symbol or text,
And so Kulan crouched low, knees bent,
Buttocks almost touching the ground, little energy spent.

His spear taken good grip of and poised in a throwing stance,
Kulan moved around, then stood silently, to glance and glance,
Before the survivors, a grimace of anger portrayed upon is face,
The spear leveraged in Wiebbe's direction, as though to disgrace.

HOLLANDIA NOVA, 1712

A knife suddenly appeared out of the blue,
Through the air, with great precision, it flew,
Penetrating deep the stomach of Kulan, a great knock,
The look upon the native's face was one of great shock.

Bewildered he looked up and saw Seebaer standing there,
Behind the other four, opened mouth of death, he did stare,
Nioka, Daku and Pindara,
Woorin, and the native Nioka.

All promptly readied their spears and pressed the survivors,
Voicing their anger, this act of betrayal from these… tumours,
The rudeness of this unprovoked attack,
This slap in the face, this great drawback.

"No! Stop!" yelled Cornelis as he and Joannes came running,
Up from the rear so fast, hearts strumming,
Followed by Barwon and Kalti, another two aboriginals,
White hands flying about, gifting their halting signals.

The stirred emotions of the other five were abated,
But only slightly - no need to be stated,
Vengeance had filled their mind,
Solace would be hard to find.

Ariaen, Wiebbe and Pieter could not believe their eyes,
Nor could Willem, the murder of a native, on whom much relies,
Seebaer endangering their lives, as though each meant nothing,
Committing the most heinous sin, Willem's heart now writhing.

It was clear, all of it, that they were about to meet their end,
Unless reprisal was performed, and their lives they must defend,
The presence of Cornelis and Joannes was proof beyond doubt,
That the natives were friendly, with a relationship to sprout.

They had given food and shown courage,
And Kulan denied future suffrage,
To be struck down for the whims of a single man,
A senseless death, against everyone's good plan.

Ariaen pulled the knife that he carried from his waist belt,
And did the one and only thing that his heart truly felt,
Within the blink of an eye rushed to Seebaer to penetrate,
To dig his knife deep within his flesh, filled with much hate.

The facial grimace of Seebaer was different,
Compared to that of Kulan's, it was more apparent,
Seebaer's grimace was of horror and pain,
His 'no-good' name now forever forbidden, a great stain.

The noise from the cliff,
No raff but much riff,
The ocean crashing about,
Gave freely its spirit, its shout.

Hard to hear from distance,
This current grievance,
And hidden by appearance,
Was the meaning of the dance.

The commotion all around was full of emotion, slow to end,
The aboriginals had congregated round their fallen friend,
Then Jan came to view, having crouched behind some bush,
To escape the horrors of being eaten alive, he remained hush.

He had believed Seebaer to the fullest, he understood,
It was true what he said, and now he knew, as he should,
Understood what it meant to be a flesh-eating native,
But he was wrong, didn't know it, none of it was relative.

Cornelis and Joannes did well,
As the seconds fell,
Showing they cared for the dead,
But within, filled with dread.

Kulan was dead,
And Seebaer of life no thread,
It was this alone that settled the calamity of the situation,
To bring to a simmer the built up frustration.

Wiebbe had pulled the bloodied knife from Seebaer as he fell,
Holding the blade he moved slowly to Narrah, to silently tell,
He held the knife out and offered it to him,
The blade blood-soaked from the fallen victim.

"No!" yelled Jan from the rear. "What are you doing; this treason?
Are you mad? You're insane; stupid beyond all comprehension."
He turned and started to run, running towards the cliff of the coast,
And at its edge leaped into the air, fell to his death, never to roast.

He was so sure, so sure of mind,
That they were to be eaten, the natives to grind,
Grind their bones, mix this with their flesh,
For a meal to be made of them, to be well mesh.

His mind was corrupted,
His thinking severely disrupted,
He failed to see what the others had seen,
Had believed Seebaer not dirty, but clean.

The afternoon had finally arrived, the sun seeking the horizon,
A fire blazed in all its glory, the men seated, victory emblazon,
They sat, not in groups of white and black,
But on equal terms, mixed: of friendship, no lack.

Said Ariaen: "I still can't believe that you're alive,"
"Yes," Cornelis agreed, "and here we are, to live and thrive,
Hard to believe that we fell in with such good fortune,
Now members of this great commune."

"We've had plenty to eat since Barwon found us,
He and Kalti, more than happy to give aid and with little fuss,
"You know them by name," said Pieter, "That's impressive."
"We've learnt a lot already, and believe their clan to be extensive."

"We haven't seen their main camp as yet,
But I believe it won't be long now before others are met."
"How do you know?" asked Wiebbe. "Is it just heart's desire?"
Asked Cornelis: "Do you see any women sitting around the fire?"

"What are they talking about?" asked Barwon, unsure,
"I don't know," said Kalti, looking into Cornelis' eyes, the allure,
"What are you talking about, Cornelis, do you know?"
Answered Cornelis. "He heard his name called just now."

"Ask him about the women," prodded Wiebbe with interest,
"Where are the women," asked Cornelis for the rest,
With hand shaping the cup of a woman's breast,
His hands held at his chest."

"Ahhh," said Barwon, *"He wants a woman, this he admits."*
"Then that confirms it all," said Kalti. *"They're not spirits,*
Maybe we should get them a woman,
Each and every man."

Asked Barwon, talking of Willem: *"Including the small one?"*
"Especially him," answered Kalti. *"He should not be alone,*
For us, the Malgana, the time for marriage is near,
We'll pass the word with none to fear."

"The Yinggarda have an agreement with the Nanda already,
Having been struck, we must now confirm it and stand steady."
Said Narrah: *"The Yinggarda won't have room for them,*
Though for the Nanda I think this is no problem."

"They're different," insisted Barwon. *"Maybe we can learn,*
A man that can float on water in a craft is not one to spurn."
"Well," said Nioka. *"They come from somewhere,*
A place that can't be seen, a place with people of skin so fair."

Barwon looked into Cornelis' eyes, *"Later we can talk,*
Talk of women, when the sun crosses the sky after a short walk."
He indicated direction with lips; arm, the movement of the sun,
"A long day's walk," said Cornelis, "I think; just one."

FOUNDATION

21st July: They slept soundly that night,
And awoke the following morning so bright,
To be provided more water and food,
The natives sitting around the fire and in a good mood.

They were talking of the day's journey,
Eating some honeycomb filled with honey,
And after an hour of relaxed feeding and contemplation,
They began their trek of unknown duration.

Wiebbe and Pieter moved over to where their poles were laid,
And the cloth used as a shelter, full of holes and frayed,
But the natives shook their heads and tried with great effort,
That they were no longer required, unable to provide any comfort.

"Leave it all here," said Joannes. "Bring the knives,
And the water containers, those things that will save lives,
Nothing more, take only what they say we need."
They nodded their heads, they all agreed.

Cornelis looked at Ariaen as he was pulling his hand away,
Saw in his eye that there was something, in pocket it lay,
He found it hard to part with an abstract of his old life, his desire,
The tinderbox. Ariaen simply smiled and threw it into the fire.

He looked upon it there, sitting in the coals, upon this new land,
To lay undisturbed for 270 years before again in the hand,
Before being found by white man, a relic of the past,
He looked up, all departing. He followed on, the very last.

The survivors had taken their first real step in cohabitation,
With the natives of this land, and with land now their relation,
And as time passed they commenced to learn, lessons to sing,
With all the clarity, the fine tuning of time, happiness to cling.

Aboriginals lived together in tribes, child, woman and man,
Made up exclusively of these family members who formed a clan,
Each clan was responsible for ensuring the well-being of the land,
They lived with it, they did not own it, always together they stand.

Men hunted with spears and fished,
Some may say, to do as they wished,
They hunted during all seasons, amidst all the yearly blossoms,
Echidnas, kangaroos, wallabies, reptiles, birds, and possums.

They used spears and boomerangs to hit, catch and kill,
Could scale trees in order to get their food, to get their fill,
Boys coming of age went with their father: to learn life's lessons,
To learn how to hunt, and make and use tools and weapons.

Women gathering the bulk of the food which was eaten daily,
They gathered medicine, seemingly happy, they did so gaily,
Girls went with their mothers to learn about the bush,
Of food and medicine; how to grind and crush.

Each tribe had an Elder who prevailed over disputes,
Decided when to move camp, of ritual they had deep roots,
They were wise in tribal knowledge, on them much relied,
Decided when boys would be initiated, and girls to be married.

It was all such an intricate network of standards and rules,
Their way of life was simple, unhurried, of people no fools,
They abided by the laws laid down, and these the whites applied,
To their everyday living, a new way of life on which they relied.

WILLEM TO WED

21st November, 1712: It had been four months since adopted,
Into the Wayle tribe, to be accepted and gifted,
The campsite was split into family groups, it was their way,
Where each maintained its own fire at the closing of day.

Ever since the episode with the metal knife,
Where Kulan was killed by Seebaer, causing much strife,
The instruments of death had been cast aside as something evil,
A valuable tool but stained and unsightly uncivil.

It was now mid-afternoon and Ariaen approached the other five,
Sitting down amongst them as Willem stoked the fire alive,
Pieter and Cornelis shaped their spear points,
And Joannes prepared for the cooking of several joints.

"Where's Wiebbe?" asked Ariaen, to the point; blunt,
"Pindara invited him out for a short hunt."
Ariaen: "Well, I have some news," looking in Willem's direction,
"What is it?" he asked. "Looking at me with such perception."

"Least of all: I've just be communicating with a man for days,
His name is Barega, and of old news he relays,
The tribe tried telling us this some time ago,
It appears that Marinus was killed by a *dingo*."

HOLLANDIA NOVA, 1712

Pieter: "I knew there was a perfect explanation."
Asked Willem: "So why are you smiling in that fashion?"
"Barega was organising a marital corroboree to the east, or south,
With the Nanda: so hard to understand his words by mouth."

"It took me awhile to understand clearly his meaning,
But now I know - I think - and I am beaming,
It's a few days' walk and all of the Malgana will attend,
We are to found, new relationship, new friend."

"And..." said Willem, under the worded cypher, feeling buried,
Ariaen smiled: "You're to be wedded, Willem, to be married."
"Married? But I'm not ready... not well; I'm still sick," he pleaded,
"It's the best thing for you; really: happiness I've really needed."

"You have a long life to live and there's only one way to live,
To be loved and for love to give,
It cannot be put off any longer,
As the days go by, with good food, you'll grow ever stronger."

"But we might be rescued," said Willem with a little confidence,
"Do you know what I believe, Willem?" said Pieter in essence,
"Once you've spent several years here with these people,
You won't want to return home; to a life so bland and simply."

"Don't talk nonsense," said Joannes. "I wouldn't care,
Even married to ten wives, I would not turn down a free fare,
I'd be firmly one aboard if I saw a ship sail past,
Whether the first man on board or the very last."

"Joannes; you'd have to live on the coast in order to see a ship,
And the coast doesn't provide all the food needed to pass your lip,
Yes, you know it's true; but life with the Malgana is great,
And I believe this to be our true fate."

"But married," said Willem again. "Whose idea was this?"
"It must have been one of the elders, something Woorak did wish,
It's so hard to understand these people sometimes, but I try,
But of their testimony and sayings I cannot rely."

"Do you know, the other day I was asking Daku 'how far',
He said *'Not long; little, short'*, of anything more I could not jar,
And then he indicated to me that it would take twelve or fourteen,
Fourteen days, I thought, not in the least very keen."

Cornelis stood up: "No, you can't. Not to the Nanda, not married,
We all like the women here, and so this idea should be parried,
I really have no dislike for them at all, and… I feel like a father,
As you all do to Willem, and I'd much prefer to stay together."

"Willem will wed and his wife will come here, it's my intention,
And as for you, young friend, I need to now mention,
One of the young women right here has taken a fancy to you,
I think the single life for you is well and truly through."

"Not Kyeema, surely," said Cornelis "Can I say nay?"
Ariaen: "Afraid not. The women folk have seen you two at play,
You should be more careful and play in the dark, you scamp,
Your manhood has revealed much to the women of this camp."

HOLLANDIA NOVA, 1712

Cornelis: "And who here isn't man enough to have a need?
I'm not the only one that's been corrupted by my own greed."
"I'm sure you're right, but this comes from the elders, their voice,
So I don't think you're going to have much choice."

"How many days did you say till—?"
"Twelve to fourteen," interrupted Pieter, "So be still."
"And we depart tomorrow," finished Ariaen, "At first light,
And Cornelis, remember your old injuries; refrain from flight."

WALGA ROCK

A first for the survivors, to move from a main camp left intact,
And it was interesting to note that this was always the fact,
Grinding stones were left upon the ground where they sat,
Shelters left as they were the night before, on ground now flat.

Sheets of bark propped up and fire smothered but left to stand,
With hot pieces of half-burnt wood carried in sand,
Ported in other wooden containers to aid in starting the next fire,
Easiness in setting up the next camp to transpire.

The days were long and hard for the survivors,
Still suffering from acclimatisation, but they were strivers,
The soles of feet bore the brunt of the heat and vegetation,
It would take time to get used to the land and its condition.

They were travelling in a direction away from the setting sun,
They continued far into the east, but also far from done,
It wasn't for the survivors to question the direction,
The path taken was weirdly peculiar but offered much fruition.

And after eleven day of walking they came upon a rock,
But its distance from them was still quite a shock,
Daku came up to Ariaen and pursed his lips, direction so set,
Pointed with his mouth towards the object of rock silhouette.

"*Walga*," said Daku, "*Walga, Walga*," towards the sun now rising,
"What's that all about?" asked Wiebbe as they continued walking,
"I'm presuming that the rock formation up ahead,
It's called Walga," announced Ariaen of what he read.

"*Walga*," said Daku again, confirming Ariaen's suspicion,
"The ceremonial grounds," said Pieter. "The place of our union,
"Maybe," agreed Ariaen, and then, "maybe not,"
And they continued with the walk, to that very spot.

Cornelis felt they were near the end of their short adventure,
For Kyeema gave him a great smile, a message, a lecture,
And he too smiled back though deep down felt unsure,
Though he felt the need for her was sincere and pure.

He didn't feel as though he was committing sin,
Possibly having children of coloured skin,
It made little difference to him, deep down,
What did it matter: white skin, black, or brown.

When they finally came upon the foot of the rock formation,
The women put about setting up camp, displaying much elation,
The men then stepped off to a place which they knew,
Where an opening existed within the rock, where shadows grew.

Ariaen and the others watched with great attentiveness,
Woorin and Daku commenced to draw, of feelings to express,
On a portion of the wall not far from the entrance but obscure,
And what they drew shocked the survivors for sure.

These two men who had lead them here were painting a picture,
A piece of art, using charcoal and red ochre, a permanent fixture,
With a mixture of many colours derived from plants so gathered,
A mural of dedication was hence, meticulously inhered.

It was a mural dedication to these strange men from across the sea,
They were accepted by the Nanda, a part of history, forever to be,
For right before them a sailing ship was being painted,
Of elegance and beauty, Ariaen felt overly sated.

A tear welled in Ariaen's eyes and Willem asked him,
"What are you crying for? Why are you feeling so dim?"
"Because we have found our way, we are at peace now,
With the land and with the people. I feel happy, not low."

"We shall never return to Europe, we have a future here,
This is now our home, and to me that is very, very clear."
Ariaen smiled at Woorin and Daku, they in turn smiled back,
This, the happiest day of Ariaen's life, of happiness never to lack.

The survivors over time were all married via great ceremony,
One of such splendour, you could not buy with VOC money,
The aboriginals did offer much more than they could ever dream,
The remaining survivors lived fruitful lives, topped with cream.

www.ingramcontent.com/pod-product-compliance
Lightning Source LLC
Chambersburg PA
CBHW020143120726
47903CB00007B/2389